CAPTIVA CHRISTMAS

CAPTIVA ISLAND SERIES
BOOK FOUR

ANNIE CABOT

CABOT PUBLISHING GROUP

ISBN ebook, 978-1-7377321-6-7

ISBN paperback, 978-1-7377321-7-4

Cover Design by Marianne Nowicki, Premade Ebook Cover Shop

For the latest information on new book releases and special giveaways, click here to be added to my list.

PROLOGUE

*L*auren Phillips panicked as she stood at the top of the escalator. Descending into the throng of Christmas shoppers, she pulled a tissue from her coat pocket and blew her nose. She'd been fighting a cold for several days, but now, just when she needed her strength the most, she melted into the crowd with little energy and a red nose.

Christmas music played over the store's speakers as she pushed through the crowd. The line leaving the building was as long as the line for the lady's room. Eyeing a chair near the entrance, she sat and waited for the strength to walk to the mall garage.

Bundled up against the cold, she regretted her selection of layered clothing that she was unable to remove in the store. She watched the line continue to move like a conveyer belt. As people entered the revolving door, more were added to the line. She'd have to get up and attack this situation with all the courage she could muster. It was, in fact, the only way out.

She walked to the end of the line and suddenly wondered if she'd be able to get through the doors with all her shopping bags. As she approached the front of the line, a man carrying nothing but a briefcase directed her to another door that had just been unlocked.

He held the door open for her. "Please, come this way."

Lauren turned sideways to get through and laughed at her predicament. She suddenly saw the humor in her situation and wondered if the man had thought she was crazy and took pity on her.

His British accent, startling blue eyes, and pleasant demeanor made her wish she looked more appealing. As it was, all she could do was thank him for his help.

"Thank you so much. For a minute, I didn't think I'd get out of there alive."

"You did look a bit frazzled. I'm happy to be of service. I guess you could say that I was in the right place at the right time. Will you be all right now, or do you need help getting to your car? The snow is coming down quite heavily."

Lauren looked past him and searched for the garage.

"I parked my car in the garage across the street. At least I think it's across the street. This snow is blinding."

He took a couple of her bags and then her elbow and together they walked toward the garage. Once inside, they shook the snow off their coats and tried to find her car.

"I have one of those little alarms on my key. It's supposed to help me find the car. I've never used it before so I've no idea if it works."

"Let's give it a try, shall we?"

Lauren placed the remaining bags on the ground and looked inside her handbag, searching for her keys. When she found them, she pressed the alarm button, and her car flashed its headlights and the alarm beeped on and off.

"There it is."

They gathered the bags and walked to the car. Lauren couldn't help but wonder who this man was. She had no right to ask him anything, but her curiosity got the better of her.

"So, am I allowed to ask a little about the man who rescued me?"

He laughed. "Oh, hardly a rescue, but forgive me. My name is Callum Foster. I'm headed to my hotel after a business meeting. Silly me, I thought I'd make a stop into the store to pick up a few Christmas gifts for family. I changed my mind when I saw the crowd. Perhaps another day. I'm very pleased to meet you."

Lauren put her bags inside the car and then closed the door.

"Lauren Phillips, it's nice to meet you as well." She extended her hand, and they shook. He didn't let go and seemed to want more time with her.

"I'm sure after all this you want to get home, but I wonder if you might be interested in having a drink or something, tea perhaps?"

She wanted nothing more in that moment but thought better of it. She could tell that he seemed embarrassed by the offer.

"I'm sorry, that was rather forward of me. It's just that I don't know anyone here, at least not yet, and I could use a friend."

"I don't understand."

"My firm is sending me to our Boston office and so I'm in the process of looking for a place to buy and, well, all that moving to America entails."

Lauren saw the opportunity.

"What kind of place are you looking for? Is it just you or do you have a family?"

"It's just me. It's hard to make a long-term commitment with someone when you travel so often. I'll be working out of the Boston location but will continue traveling back and forth to the UK. I'm not sure what I'm looking for exactly except to say that it shouldn't be a place that needs work. I need something I can move into right away."

Lauren reached into her wallet and pulled out her business card.

"It just so happens that I own a real estate company. I'd be happy to help you find something that will work for your situation."

He looked at the card. "Lauren Phillips. Brilliant. It looks like you might have saved my life as well today. What shall we do to celebrate?"

Lauren didn't want to hurt his feelings, but she had to get back to her husband and two daughters who were waiting for her at home.

"My husband will be worried about me, especially in this weather. Thank you so much for helping me, and for the offer to have tea, but I must decline."

"Right. Of course, you must get home. Well then, thank you again for giving me your card. I'll be ringing you first thing Monday morning if that's all right with you. We can talk about the details then. Would you be willing to meet over coffee on Monday?"

After turning him down once, she didn't have the heart to say no. It wasn't official, but he more than likely would be her client by then. There was nothing inappropriate about having coffee with a client, after all.

"Of course. That will be fine."

"I'll see you then, Lauren. Be careful driving home."

She waved to him as she pulled out of the garage and onto the road. The snowflakes were large and coming down at a steady pace.

With four inches on the ground, it bothered Lauren that Jeff hadn't at least called her cell phone to see if she was all right. She'd been gone for hours, and if she wasn't careful, might easily skid off the road. Driving slowly, the only sound she could hear was the wiper blades streaking across the windshield.

Watching the brake lights in front of her, she used them as a guide to stay in her lane. She tried not to be upset at her husband's lack of concern for her safety and focused on the ride home. She knew what she'd find as soon as she walked in the front door. No one would great her or even say hello. Everyone would be busy with their own interests and odds were she'd find Jeff laying on the sofa watching a Bruins game.

Maybe turning down tea with Callum Foster was a mistake.

At least he'd be someone interested in her. She wouldn't be invisible to him. He'd make her feel that her real estate business success was something to feel proud of instead of ashamed. Whatever awaited her at home, there was always Monday morning, and the intriguing life of a British gentleman to look forward to.

CHAPTER 1

*M*aggie Wheeler sat on the inn's porch swing and listened to the waves hitting the shore. Looking at the carriage house, she smiled, thinking of her husband, Paolo curled up on his side, enjoying several more hours of sleep.

It was three o'clock in the morning when she lay staring at the alarm clock, fighting the need for fresh air. It didn't take long before she gave in and, grabbing her bathrobe, walked down the stairs and across the driveway to the Key Lime Garden Inn.

She couldn't shake the uneasy feeling that something was wrong. As far as she could tell all of her children were healthy and doing well, and with three guest rooms filled, nothing about the inn seemed amiss. And yet, a foreboding had her stomach in knots. The feeling stayed with her for the better part of an hour before her husband joined her on the porch.

"Maggie, is everything all right? I reached over for you and when you weren't there, I got scared."

Maggie reached for Paolo and pulled him next to her. She snuggled against his warm body and whispered,

"I'm fine. I just couldn't sleep. Keep your voice down or the

7

others will wake. The last thing I want is to have our guests find me in my bathrobe."

The faint smell of Paolo's cologne from the night before settled her nerves. Being in his arms and feeling his strength always comforted her whenever she felt stress, but this feeling was something else, and she longed to find its cause.

"Paolo, what do you think about having everyone come down for Christmas? I'm thinking all the kids and grandkids, everyone."

"I think it's ambitious. You know how much work it takes to coordinate their schedules. Now, with the grandchildren's school to consider, it might be difficult."

Maggie sat up straight and looked at him. "We've had family members down here several times already without issue. What makes you think this would be any different?"

"Because my love, I know you. The last time the whole family was on the island was when you moved down here two years ago. A lot has happened since then and there are more people to consider. I know you won't be happy unless every single person shows up for the holiday. I just don't want you to get your hopes up."

Paolo was right. It was typical for Maggie to only see the positive. It was a perspective she'd applied throughout her life to avoid unpleasant confrontations, but it had a way of backfiring on her.

For now, she held steady to the belief that all would turn out exactly as she planned. No Grinch would cloud the image of her entire family standing around a large Christmas tree, even if that Grinch was her husband.

Paolo ran his hand up and down her arm and then squeezed her tight.

"How about we go back to bed and talk about this tomorrow?"

Maggie nodded. They got up from the swing, careful not to

wake their guests. Arm in arm they walked back to the carriage house. Maggie climbed back under the comforter, but she knew sleep would not come.

She didn't want Paolo to worry but, whatever was troubling her, she was convinced it would be solved by celebrating the holiday with her family. Christmas on Captiva Island surrounded by the people she loved most in the world was sure to quell her fears, and as soon as the sun came up she'd get her journal and start planning. She had three weeks before her family's traditional Christmas Eve party. Not much time for her children to book flights if they were lucky enough to find available seats at all.

Maggie sighed and tried to relax but it was no use. She wouldn't rest easy until her plan was underway and could start decorating the inn with all the Christmas trimmings. She wiggled her toes under the comforter and looked at the clock on her nightstand, willing the night away.

Chelsea Marsden marched into the kitchen of the Key Lime Garden Inn and immediately made her way to the coffee pot.

"And a very good morning to you, too," Maggie said.

"I wouldn't know, I haven't had my coffee yet."

Maggie continued slicing pieces of her mushroom and onion quiche and waited for Chelsea to share what was on her mind.

"Chelsea, it's never good when you're quiet. Are you going to make me wait or am I going to have to bribe you with something better than my quiche?"

"I'm sorry, Maggie. I'm not sure whether I'm mad or just worried. Sebastian is moving to Paris."

Stunned, Maggie reached for Chelsea.

"Oh, honey, I'm so sorry. When?"

"He's not selling his house on Captiva, it's just that after all this time he never mentioned he also had a house in France. I didn't realize that's where he was born and spent most of his childhood. His mother was born in Bernay, Normandy. He said that once he and I started dating, he put the Paris home on hold. Now, he wants to return for a while."

"Well, that's not terrible, is it? I'd love to travel to Paris. I'm jealous."

"Maggie, you don't understand. When he goes to Paris, he's there for months at a time. This time he wants to be there until June. That's six months. I can't go to Paris for six months."

"I assume he's asked you?"

Chelsea sipped her coffee and nodded. "He did."

"And?"

"I told him I needed to think about it. I love living on Captiva. I don't think I'd be happy living anywhere else."

Maggie put a piece of the quiche on a plate and handed it to Chelsea. "Who said you have to live in Paris for the whole six months? Why not come and go as you wish? It's not like the two of you are married or planning to date other people. You have an arrangement that works, so why change that?"

Chelsea's face lit up as if Maggie had said something amazing.

"Why didn't I think of that? I guess I could do that if I wanted. Maybe even my BFF would go with me one of those times."

Now it was Maggie's face that lit up. "Oh, my goodness, I'd love that. Now that I think of it wouldn't you have to get a special visa to stay there that long?"

Chelsea didn't answer her but instead grabbed Maggie's arm in panic. Her voice, barely a whisper, she struggled to understand her situation.

"Oh, Maggie. What if this is Sebastian's way of telling me he wants to be more serious. I mean can a proposal be that far behind?"

Maggie stirred the cream in her coffee and smiled.

"Would that be so bad? How do you feel about getting married again?"

Chelsea looked like she'd just been given terrible news.

"Don't get me wrong, I love Sebastian, and I'm not scared of marriage or anything like that. Honestly, it hasn't been that long since I let myself fall in love again. These past few months have been great. It's like we've settled in as a couple and there isn't anything more to struggle with. I'm content with things exactly as they are."

"Then you've nothing to worry about. I'm sure Sebastian feels the same way you do."

Chelsea chewed her quiche and nodded.

"Let's hope so. The last thing I want is an ultimatum. If he pushes me, we're going to have a problem."

Maggie felt for her friend. Navigating a second chance at love later in life was tricky. Two people wanting the same things out of life was rare. All she could do was support Chelsea and hope that she'd be as lucky as she and Paolo had been.

If things didn't go well for Chelsea and Sebastian, Maggie needed to prepare herself. She made a mental note to make the Key Limetini ingredients front and center in the cabinet. Chelsea's famous signature drink, and a shoulder to cry on usually got Chelsea through any unpleasant situation.

"What about you?"

"Huh?"

"Maggie, I can see it in your eyes that something's on your mind. I don't usually have to guess, but this time I think I do. Let's see…Christopher and Becca are doing great. Beth's job is keeping her busy and her relationship with Gabriel seems to be doing well. Sarah's in her second trimester and everyone at her house is healthy and happy. I think it's got to either be Michael and Brea or Lauren and Jeff. It's a toss-up, but I'm going to guess it's Lauren and Jeff."

Maggie both loved and hated the way her friend could solve

any mystery. The mention of Lauren's marriage gave Maggie the same uneasy feeling she had in the middle of the night. Giving any credibility to Chelsea's guess scared her and so she did the best she could to change the subject.

"Chelsea, everyone is fine. You're making a big deal about nothing. I'm probably a little tired, that's all. I woke up around two-thirty and couldn't get back to sleep so I sat out on the porch for a while. Maybe we should have some fresh cantaloupe that I cut up earlier. It's really juicy."

"Ah-ha. I knew it. Did you make yourself a cup of tea? That's usually a really good clue."

"Oh, for heaven's sake. No. I did not make myself a cup of tea. I felt unsettled and since I was awake I thought I'd enjoy the fresh air."

Chelsea shook her head. "Nope, that's not it. I know you better than you know yourself. If you couldn't sleep, you had something on your mind. Maybe you don't even know what it is, but you should trust your intuition. What does your gut say?"

Maggie had enough of her friend's prying. It's not like she had any idea what made her so uneasy in the middle of the night, but something stirred her thinking, and nothing seemed to calm her nerves.

"My gut tells me that I need another slice of that quiche with a side of cantaloupe. Do you want another?"

Maggie didn't want to make more of her sleepless night. If they continued talking about it, there was a good chance that she'd feel worse. For now, planning the family Christmas visit to the island was all she wanted to think about.

CHAPTER 2

*L*auren watched as Jeff buttoned Olivia's coat. Their younger daughter, Lily stood next to him, waiting her turn.

"How come you button Olivia's coat first? Is it because she's older?"

"No silly. Olivia got to me before you, that's all."

Lily took that as a challenge.

"I'm going to be first next time, Livy. You'll see. I'm fast."

Jeff looked at Lauren and smiled.

Their marriage had gone through a rough patch the last few months, but moments like this one, made the bad days easily forgotten.

They'd made two beautiful children together, and Lauren couldn't forget what a wonderful father Jeff had been. Being a stay-at-home dad confused their friends, and they often had to explain their situation to those who couldn't wrap their heads around such an arrangement. It made her laugh to think of the questions she'd answered at least once a week.

"What does he do while you're away at work?"

"The same things I used to do, cooking, cleaning, helping the girls with their homework, getting them to school and after school events. We've just swapped our roles and now I work outside the home, and he works inside. We realize it's not very conventional, but it works for us."

Usually, people would nod and instead of moving on to another subject, they'd continue to probe.

"Don't you miss your children?"

Everyone seemed intent on making Lauren feel guilty. Most days, she didn't feel bad at all. Jeff had things under control and the girls didn't suffer for attention and guidance. She did miss being with them, but the cost of motherhood had taken a toll on her that was unexpected. For all the attempts at finding balance, she was happier going to work every day. Shocked that her husband hated his job and longed to be a stay-at-home father, they'd found a family dynamic that worked. At least, she believed it was working.

Until it wasn't.

Jeff resented her for working long hours trying to build her real estate business. When she'd finally make it home, she'd spend hours on her laptop or deep in the paperwork that was strewn about the dining room table. Jeff's words continued to plague her.

"Even when you're here, you're not really here. Did you know that Lily lost a baby tooth?" and, "I specifically gave you the date for Olivia's dance recital, and you still didn't make it."

The struggle was real, and Lauren didn't have a solution. Marriage counseling hadn't helped and after their last session, she was considering canceling any future appointments. The best they could do was to protect their girls from any trauma which meant keeping the tension between them low. Shopping for their family Christmas tree was a good start.

"We better get going before it starts to snow heavily again. They're calling for an additional six inches."

Jeff nodded and put on his coat.

"Everybody ready? Let's go. Last one in the car is a rotten egg."

Olivia shook her head and rolled her eyes.

Lauren smiled at her oldest who constantly acted like she was seven going on seventeen.

They piled into the Jeep and headed for the Christmas tree farm on the outskirts of Andover. As difficult as it was to drive through, Lauren loved watching the large snowflakes fall around them.

"Did you pack the tarp?"

Jeff nodded.

"And the rope?"

"Yes, and the saw. Why do you do that every year?"

"Do what?"

"We're halfway to the farm and you ask me if I've packed everything we need to cut down the tree. If you're going to ask, why not do it before we leave, not after?"

These were the kind of daily exchanges that dominated their communication. Every topic was dissected and scrutinized to the point of exhaustion.

Lauren didn't bother to answer him, instead, sitting quietly in the passenger seat wishing she'd never said a word.

When the farm came into view, Olivia unfastened her seatbelt.

"Olivia! Sit back and put your seatbelt on."

"Sorry, Mom. I'm so excited. I can see the lights of the farm. It must be really pretty at night. Why don't we ever get our tree at nighttime. It would be a lot prettier then."

Jeff answered her. "Because if we waited until it got dark, we wouldn't be able to see well enough to cut the tree. Besides, all the best trees are gone by then. You have to get to the farm just as they open up."

They pulled into the parking lot and while Lauren got Olivia and Lily out of the car, Jeff reached for the saw and tarp. Getting to the farm early had been a good plan. So far, there were only two other cars in the lot. Soon, the place would be swarming with shoppers dressed in layers against the cold. At least the sun was starting to peek behind the clouds.

Lily pulled on Lauren's coat. "Mommy, can I have a hot chocolate?"

Olivia joined in. "Me too?"

"You can, but first we have to pick out our tree and then we take the hayride up to the main house to pay for it and buy our wreath. That's when we get hot chocolate. Come on, let's help Daddy pick out the tree."

They followed Jeff into the forest of trees and Lauren lifted her face to the sun. Its warmth felt soothing and as much as she loved this tradition, a part of her longed to be sitting on the beach on Captiva Island. She knew the sun would once again go behind the clouds, so she hurried the girls, catching up with Jeff.

Olivia pointed to a tree. "I like this one."

Jeff looked the tree over and then at Lily. "What do you think, Lily? Do you think this is a good one?"

Lily nodded her approval, but Lauren knew the real reason was to move things along so that they could climb up on the hayride for their journey to the hot chocolate station.

Jeff cut down the tree and dropped it on the tarp. Pulling the large balsam fir along the path, he left it with a young man who gave him a ticket.

"Sir, you can either walk up to the main house or take the hayride. Just bring your ticket to the register and they'll take care of you."

Jeff thanked the boy and the four of them got in line, waiting for the horse-drawn flatbed to return to the bottom of the hill.

Lauren and Jeff helped the girls onto the hayride first and then joined them, sitting on bales of hay. Lily tried to talk to the horse, but the driver explained that she'd have to wait until they disembarked up at the main house. He promised her a private audience with the animal, and Lily beamed with excitement over the special attention.

True to his word, the man helped Lily off the hayride and walked her over to the horse. He picked her up in his arms and let her pet the animal.

"What's his name?"

"This here's Tucker."

"Hi Tucker. I'm Lily."

"Daddy, I want to pet Tucker too."

Lauren watched as Jeff brought Olivia to meet the horse. The image moved her deeply, and she couldn't stop the tears that welled in her eyes. She pulled her cell phone from her purse and called out to her family.

"Everyone says cheese."

The driver put Lily down and stopped Lauren. "You get in the picture too. I'll take one of the four of you."

"Thank you so much."

Lauren handed her cell phone to the man and joined her family.

"Get ready, say cheese."

In unison they all yelled, "Cheese."

The driver handed the phone back to Lauren. "There you go. I'm off to get the next group, but I'll see you on the return."

They watched him lift the reigns and turn in the circular drive following a path back to where they started.

Jeff put his gloved hands together and moved them back and forth.

"Let's get inside and have some of that delicious hot chocolate."

Lauren watched as Jeff and the girls made their way inside the barn. She sighed, wishing every day could be like this one. She wondered how many more opportunities they would get to feel normal and without the dreaded fear that had permeated every aspect of their lives.

However much longer they had before the shoe dropped, she didn't know. She took a deep breath and pushed thoughts of anything other than holiday decorating aside. No sense thinking about what tomorrow might bring when today was staring her in the face.

Lauren wasted little time getting to her office early on Monday morning. It would be at least another hour before her employees, Brian and Nell, walked through the door. Plenty of time to plan for her meeting with Callum Foster. Without knowing exactly what he was looking for, she decided to pull up several listings that might appeal to him and printed their details.

She had no idea when he would call, or if he would. After all, he was a complete stranger and although a seemingly kind gentleman, could easily have made a promise he never intended to keep. However, something deep inside convinced her that their time in the mall shopping garage wasn't the last time she'd see him.

The real estate office didn't open for another hour, and she worried she might miss his phone call, so she disconnected the voice mail feature on the office phones.

Every time the phone rang, she jumped. When Brian and Nell walked in exactly at nine o'clock, Callum still hadn't called.

"Good morning. Did you guys have a nice weekend?"

Brian looked like he hadn't slept in days. "If you call getting up several times in the night to attend to Alison two nights in a row, a nice weekend, then yes, I had lots of fun."

Lauren laughed at him. "I remember those days, and you would probably think I'm crazy when I tell you that I miss them."

On his way to the kitchen, he nodded. "You're right. I think you're crazy."

"How about you, Nell? What did you do?"

Nell looked as though she had a secret. She beamed and flashed her left hand in front of Lauren.

"Oh, my goodness. You got engaged?"

Nell squealed and Brian came running back to join them.

"I did. Damien proposed to me Saturday night at the Bistro. It was so romantic. He got down on one knee and everything. He even had his friend hide out in the back of the restaurant with a camera. I've got the whole thing on my cell phone. Want to see?"

Lauren, Nell and Brian had their heads together admiring the large diamond when the front door opened, and Callum Foster walked in.

"Oh, hello."

"I'm sorry, have I interrupted something? I can come back later if you'd rather."

"No. Not at all. I wasn't expecting you."

"Should we do this another time?"

Lauren suddenly realized her shock at seeing Callum in person must have appeared as though he'd done something wrong. She needed to put on her professional real estate face and stop acting like a love-struck teenager.

"I'm glad you stopped in. Please, won't you come into my office. Let's see if we can find you the perfect home. If I understood you correctly, you're looking for a property to buy, not rent. Is that right?"

Callum took the seat in front of Lauren's desk and dropped his briefcase on the floor.

"Yes, that's right, but first let me say that I'm glad to see you got home with no troubles. The snow was coming down rather suddenly the other day and I'd hoped you made it home without incident."

"Leaving the mall when I did was a good idea. I think I might have been stranded there if I'd waited any longer."

His blue eyes stared into hers. "I'd have been rather happy if you had. Maybe I would have been able to talk you into having that drink or perhaps even dinner with me."

Lauren could feel her face getting warm and worried that Callum could see her blush. Their conversation was traveling in uncharted waters, and she needed to get back on course as quickly as possible.

"Why don't you tell me a bit about what you're looking for. I've already pulled several attractive listings, but I don't want to waste your time looking at any of them if it's not entirely what you want. How many bedrooms and bathrooms would you need?"

Callum sat back in his chair and smiled.

"As I mentioned, at present I'm single and without a significant other, but I also know that my situation may change in the future. I best be prepared for that, wouldn't you say?"

Everything about Callum made Lauren feel uneasy. She hadn't done anything wrong, and yet, she couldn't shake the feeling that spending time with him was a mistake. As soon as possible, she decided that her newly engaged employee sitting out front would be better suited to show properties to Callum. She made a note to talk to Nell about it.

How to approach the subject with him, however, she didn't know, but she couldn't worry about that now. Keeping her distance from the man was more important than keeping the client. If he found another real estate company to meet his needs, so be it. Lauren had another, more urgent relationship to focus on, even if it was too late to repair.

CHAPTER 3

*M*aggie had two hours before her lunch-bunch virtual get-together. Knowing Chelsea, she'd show up an hour early. With that in mind, Maggie made a pot of tea, and since all her guests were elsewhere, decided to sit on the porch and call each of her children about her plans for Christmas.

The more time she'd spent with the idea, the better she felt about it, and couldn't wait to hear her family get equally excited. She called Sarah first since she already lived on Sanibel and would be the one most likely to accept the invitation.

"Hey, Mom. I was just going to call you."

"Oh, what about?"

"Do I need a reason? I just wanted to hear my mother's voice."

"Oh, that's sweet. Well, from one mother to another, how are you feeling?"

"Better than the first few weeks that's for sure. No more nausea and I've got tons of energy. It's coming in handy because I've been so involved with the domestic violence women's shelter benefit, I can't afford to slow down now. What's new over at your place?"

"That's why I'm calling. I've got an idea I thought I'd run by you. What do you think about having the whole family down for Christmas?"

"Oh, Mom. I don't know. Have you talked to anyone besides me? It's sort of last minute."

"I haven't called anyone yet. You're the first. I thought I'd get your opinion before I got in touch with the others. You and Trevor can make it Christmas Eve, right?"

There was a hesitance in Sarah's voice. Maggie couldn't afford to lose the one vote in her favor right out of the gate.

"The plan is to stop by the inn and visit with you and Paolo, and then we're due at Trevor's parents' home in Cape Coral and there until it's bedtime. Don't worry, we'll be there, it's just that you shouldn't depend on us to stay very long."

Maggie was disappointed already. Was it too much to ask to have all her children around her on their most special night?

"Sarah, I understand. This happens all the time when people get married. You've got your in-laws to think about. Not to mention you're going to want to have your children get equal time with both sets of grandparents. Promise me you'll stay as long as possible, and we'll get tons of pictures."

"I promise. Good luck calling everyone and let me know how you make out. I'd love nothing more than to have as many family members surrounding Noah and Sophia as possible. I'm in your corner. Talk to you later. Love you."

"Love you, too, honey."

Maggie sighed and wondered if Paolo was right that she best not get her hopes up. She called Christopher who picked up his phone after only one ring.

"How's my favorite mother?"

"Very funny, and I'm fine thank you. How are you and Becca?"

"Things are great up here. Becca's been studying around the clock and when she doesn't have her nose in her books, she's racing me all the way to heartbreak hill."

"So, the prosthetic blade is working well?"

"Yeah. It took me a bit to get used to it, and I'm still doing physical therapy, but otherwise everything is working just as planned…for once."

"Chris, I'm calling because I want to invite everyone down for Christmas, the whole family. We haven't been together for the holiday in three years. I think it's important that we keep some of our traditions."

"Traditions? You mean Christmas Eve? Mom, you do know you're in Florida, right? How are we going to sing White Christmas down there?"

"Christopher Wheeler. Be serious. This is important to me."

"Ok, Mom. Listen, I can't promise anything. It all depends on Becca. Trying to get her to do anything but study is nearly impossible. I'll see what I can do, but just in case, don't count on us until you hear from me."

"That's fine. Do your best to convince her. I miss you two."

"You can't possibly miss that grumpy guy who used to live in your downstairs bedroom, can you?"

"Yes, even him. I miss everything about my boy."

Maggie didn't want to cry, but she was realizing that she had little control over her children's lives any longer."

"I've got to go, Mom. I'm late for Summit Compass. Love you lots."

"Bye honey, I love you too. Say hi to Becca."

Maggie ended the call and chewed on her nail, a habit that had long ago ended but recently started up again. When she realized it, she pulled her finger out of her mouth and slammed shut the cover of her journal. She had three more to contact but was suddenly afraid to place another call. She felt like her children were slipping away from her, and there was little she could do about it. They didn't need her anymore and that pained her more than anything.

When she reached Michael's cell phone, his voicemail

message answered. She left him a message and decided to call his wife Brea.

"Hi, Maggie. So nice to hear from you. I wish I could talk, but I'm just about to head out to a dentist appointment. Did you want to talk to Michael? He's at work so you could leave him a message."

"I'm well, Brea. Everyone ok at your house?"

"Yes, everyone is fine. I'll let Michael know that you called. I've got to run. Take care, Maggie."

Maggie barely had a chance to ask Brea anything before she rushed her off the phone. It was probably for the best since she'd have better luck talking to her son instead. Hopefully, Michael would call her back soon.

Next on her list was Beth, and even though her daughter was probably at work, Maggie had no choice but to call her there. Christmas was only a little more than three weeks away, and they were already cutting it close. Beth's phone rang several times before she picked up.

"Mom. Is everything all right? You don't usually call me when I'm at the office."

"Yes, of course. Things are fine here. How about you?"

Beth sounded happy and glad to hear from her which made Maggie feel better.

"I'm doing great. Having Chris stay with me has been awesome. I never minded living alone, but now that he's here I wouldn't want it any other way. Can you imagine me saying how much I love being around my little brother? So, tell me what's going on?"

"Beth, I know you and Gabriel are busy with your careers, but I was hoping that since we haven't had a real family Christmas in a few years, that you all would come down to Florida so we can celebrate the holiday together. What do you say?"

Beth's cheerful voice changed, and Maggie knew immediately that Beth was about to say something she didn't want to hear.

"Oh, Mom. I wish we could come down. It's beautiful on Captiva, and of course you know how much I miss you."

"But?"

"But this is our first Christmas together and we were planning a bunch of stuff…you know…romantic things like taking a sleigh ride, ice skating on the Public Gardens, walking around Boston Common enjoying the lights—that kind of stuff."

Even though Beth couldn't see her, Maggie nodded her head.

"I understand, honey. You and Gabriel will want to start your own traditions, and you should. Don't worry about a thing. You do what you want to do and have fun."

"Mom, are you sure? I feel terrible."

"Beth you have nothing to feel terrible about. Times change and we have to change with them, right? There will be other Christmases."

"Thanks, Mom. I knew you'd understand. By the way, if you were thinking of inviting Lauren and Jeff down, I wouldn't bother. Things are pretty dicey over at their house. Chris and I have had a few dinners at their house and the tension is awful. I hate to say it, but after all these months of them fighting, I thought things would settle down and they'd fix whatever is wrong. Instead, it feels like both of them have given up trying."

"Oh, Beth. I hate hearing this. I've been thinking about them ever since Sarah's wedding. I thought by now…"

"I know, Mom. I feel the same. Anyway, I've got to run. Say hello to Paolo for me."

When she ended the call Maggie had to wonder if there could ever be another Christmas where all of her children would gather around her tree. Memories from the past came flooding back and her heart hurt. It seemed that nothing would ever be the same for the Wheeler family. The sooner she accepted that the better for everyone going forward.

❄

Chelsea pulled her car up in front of Sebastian's home and grabbed her umbrella. It hadn't rained in weeks and so she took the downpour as an ominous sign. Taking a deep breath, she braced herself for a storm. Undeterred, she got out of her car and made her way through the raindrops and under the portico.

Opening her handbag, she found her mirror and looking into it, fluffed her hair.

Dispirited, she sighed. "Nice, Chelsea. You look like a drowned rat."

She shrugged her shoulders and put the mirror back in her bag.

"No turning back now."

Sebastian's housekeeper answered the door. "Good morning, Ms. Marsden. Can I take your jacket?"

"Yes, thank you, Elaine. Is Mr. Barlowe home? I know he wasn't expecting me."

"Yes, he's in his study. Shall I take you to him?"

"No. I know the way."

Sebastian's home was unlike any Chelsea had seen on the island. She imagined there were others like it among the wealthy communities of Sanibel and the exclusive, hidden-away homes on Captiva, but she'd never seen the inside any of them. Expansive and uncluttered, Sebastian's home nevertheless was inviting.

Clean, turquoise, and white everywhere she looked, Chelsea thought it an extension of the sea—the kind of place only mermaids lived.

When she opened the door to his study, Sebastian sat in the corner of the room, reading a book. When he saw her, he waved for her to join him.

"Chelsea! This is a wonderful surprise. I was just thinking of you."

She kissed his cheek and sat across from him.

"You mean there's something in that book that made you think of me?"

He laughed and closed the book holding it up for her to see. *Moving to Paris. Everything You Need to Know.*

"I guess you could say that. I can't wait to show you around, but I picked this book up for you, actually."

He handed the book to her and she felt it a perfect opening to talk about her concerns.

"Thank you, Sebastian. Speaking of Paris, I came here this morning to talk about that. I honestly don't think I can commit to such a long time there. I've been thinking about what it would be like to live so far away from everything I love here. I'm settled on Captiva. It's my home, at least it's become my home ever since Carl died. Living on the island permanently has always been my dream, and it took me years to get here. This is where my husband died, and it is where I will die."

She could tell from the look on his face that he was disappointed.

"Chelsea, I don't want you to come with me to Paris as my girlfriend. I want you to be my wife. I know we've danced around this subject for a while now, but I think it's time we talked seriously about this."

She knew this discussion was inevitable and hated that it had almost come to an ultimatum, but he was right, she needed to be straight with him.

"I can't marry you, Sebastian. It's not that I don't love you, because I do. It's taken me a bit to get used to having a man in my life again, and I've loved every minute of being with you. I don't want our relationship to end, but if we continue, it will have to be as it has been. If you feel that you don't want me to come to Paris unless we're husband and wife, then I'm going to have to decline. I won't marry again, and I won't change my mind about this. I hope you will understand."

As worried as she had been leading up to this confrontation, Chelsea immediately felt the weight of it float away. She'd finally said out loud what she'd wanted to say for months. Calling

Sebastian her boyfriend seemed silly at her age, but there was no other role he could play in her life.

He took her hand in his.

"Then will you let me show you Paris as the most important woman in my life? Come for as long as you wish. I won't pressure you to stay longer than you want to, but I'm not willing to lose what we have. I love you, Chelsea. I'll be whatever you want me to be. I do want to live in my home in France for several months —six, maybe less, but you come and stay as long as you like. It will be my honor to show you a little of the world I grew up in. Let me surround you with the beauty that is Paris. Say you'll come."

Sebastian's proposal stunned her. Certain they were about to end their relationship, she was unprepared for his offer. She'd stayed true to her convictions regardless of the cost, and Sebastian had willingly accepted her choice.

She leaned in close to him. Placing her hand on his face she kissed him. She pulled back and looked into his eyes.

"Thank you for understanding my feelings. I've always wanted to see Paris. I'd love to go with you, when do we leave?"

CHAPTER 4

*I*f Captiva Island had a Mayor, Byron Jameson would serve several terms with no one to oppose him. The island's original busy-body, Byron knew all the residents and even a few tourists who made the island their annual vacation home. He'd grown up in southwest Florida, but once retired, made Captiva Island his home.

When he first moved to the island he took a job as golf cart shuttle driver for the South Seas Resort. While transporting residents around the resort he'd talk about the history of the island and the original residents as if he'd known them personally. More than once he kept a person on the cart longer than they wanted, but once Byron started talking, it was hard to get away from him.

Being nosy paid off for Byron as he paid attention when wealthy vacationers talked about their investments and made changes to his own portfolio in turn. Rumor was that Byron was one of the wealthiest men on the island, a fable he no doubt started.

He knew everyone's secrets, and most couldn't tell if he was a harmless old man or someone to be feared, and that was exactly how he liked it. Understanding the importance of optics, Byron continued to drive around the island in his golf cart, looking like he was doing nothing more than enjoying the sun and sand all the while sticking his nose in other people's business.

When Maggie opened the Key Lime Garden Inn, Byron was one of her first visitors. Since that time, he'd stop by to chat and share a bit of gossip that he wanted passed around. He preferred to visit the inn when Chelsea was there because he knew that she would pass on whatever new story he wanted circulated. Maggie wouldn't indulge the man, but she loved his colorful demeanor and welcomed him into her kitchen in the early morning breakfast hours.

"Good morning, Byron."

"Lovely Day, Ms. Moretti. Any chance I might get a scone this morning?"

Maggie laughed and pulled out a chair. "Have a seat. I was just about to take them out of the oven."

"Knock, Knock. How about a plate for your BFF?"

Byron jumped up from his chair and opened the backdoor.

"My goodness, what a chivalrous gentleman you are Mr. Jameson."

"You know how much I love seeing you, Chelsea. Now, my day is perfect."

Bryon pulled out a chair for Chelsea and then sat across from her.

Amused, Maggie watched them flirt with each other.

"Chelsea, why don't you leave that awful Mr. Barlowe and run away with me?"

"Oh, I don't know, Byron. I think you're too young for me. I'm not sure I could keep up."

Maggie carried a plate with several warm scones to the table. "How about some coffee? Bryon, would you like a cup?"

"Oh no, not for me. I've already had two. If I have any more my golf cart will be pulled over for speeding. I'll just have a scone Maggie dear."

Maggie didn't have to ask Chelsea. Without her morning coffee, her friend couldn't function. She poured Chelsea a cup and placed the cream and sugar on the table.

With a mouth full of scone, Byron tried to talk. "We've finished with the decorations on Andy Rosse, now we're almost ready for the Christmas Festival. I wanted to stop by and ask you if you need any help decorating the inn. I've got lots of guys willing to help you and Mr. Moretti if you want."

Maggie understood the subtle message. The Key Lime Garden Inn didn't have any Christmas lights outside, a fact that didn't go unnoticed by the islanders, and therefore, Byron. It wasn't that Maggie didn't want the lights; it was just that this year she didn't feel like celebrating very much. She couldn't explain it to anyone, but this Christmas she felt more like Scrooge than one of Santa's helpers.

"No. We don't need any help. We've just been busy that's all. The inn sits so far back off the road, it can't possibly bother anyone that its Christmas lights are missing. Can it?"

She could tell that Byron didn't want to hurt her feelings, but his face made clear what his wishes were.

"I'll get the lights up right away, Byron. Heaven help the island if the inn goes a Christmas without holiday lights."

Byron smiled and nodded, finishing his scone. As soon as he was done, he walked to the front of the inn instead of leaving out the back. It only took a minute before Maggie understood why.

"Maggie! You don't have your Christmas tree up yet. What happened? Where's your tree?"

Maggie rolled her eyes at Chelsea who was trying not to laugh.

"We haven't shopped for our tree just yet, Byron. Like I said before, we've been busy."

He came toward her and took her hands in his.

"Maggie. At this time of year, nothing is more important than sharing the holiday spirit with your guests. I have to imagine that one of the reasons they've come to the island this time of year is to celebrate Christmas here. It falls to us residents to present a beautiful and picture-perfect Christmas to them. We don't want them going home thinking we're all Scrooges now do we?"

The image of Byron wearing a hat with jingle bells on the end with barely covered elf ears made Maggie laugh out loud. Byron took her laughter as a sign that she was starting to get on board with welcoming the Christmas spirit into the inn.

Composing herself, she answered him, "No. Of course not. I'll talk to Mr. Moretti, and we'll get right on that."

He tapped her hands and then walked through the kitchen and out the back door. "You ladies have a wonderful day. Merry Christmas."

Chelsea yelled out as he left, "Ho. Ho. Ho."

Chelsea finished her breakfast and looked at Maggie.

"Are you going to wear that today?"

Maggie looked down at her clothes. She was still wearing her old gardening clothes and didn't bother to change as she baked her scones.

"You're right, I look a mess. I guess I'll talk to Paolo about the inn's decorations and then get in the shower."

"You haven't forgotten it's lunch-bunch day, have you?"

"Oh Chelsea, is that today? I completely forgot."

Maggie thought about it and changed her decorating plans.

"I guess we can decorate tomorrow. I still need Paolo to get the boxes of Christmas lights and ornaments down from the attic anyway. We're doing this over at your place, right?"

"Yup. I'm going to get back home and prepare the lunch for us. I'll set up the computer monitor like always."

"Sounds good."

Maggie started to clean the kitchen when Chelsea reached for her.

"Wait. I came over here this morning to tell you something. I didn't want to say anything when Byron was here."

Maggie put the plates in the sink and wiping her hands on a towel, returned to the table.

Chelsea looked serious and it worried Maggie.

"What is it?"

"I'm going to Paris with Sebastian right after Christmas."

Her stomach suddenly turning, Maggie didn't like the idea of her best friend leaving the island.

"Chelsea, please tell me you're not leaving Captiva Island. I don't think I could stand that."

"No, I'm not leaving for good. I'm going for a month or maybe more. I'm not exactly sure. I've decided to leave things open and make my decision about how long I'll stay after I've been there for a while. I'm only booking a one-way flight for now."

"For now? What does that mean? Are you saying that you might live in Paris?"

"Sebastian asked me to marry him, and I turned him down. I'm actually thrilled with the way things turned out."

Maggie didn't know how to react to this news.

"I'm sorry, Chelsea. I'm confused. What exactly is your plan?"

Chelsea reached for Maggie.

"I'm never leaving Captiva Island, Maggie, and I'm also never getting married again. I explained to him that this is my home and where I plan to live for the rest of my life. I explained that I'm willing to go to Paris with him for an undetermined amount of time, but that I'll be returning to Captiva a single woman. This was your idea, remember? You said I can choose to go for as long as I want."

Maggie found her breath again. Panic had set in and although

33

she wanted her friend to be happy, she couldn't stand the thought of losing Chelsea.

"You're sure, Chelsea?"

"I'm sure, and what's more I was able to tell him what I want for my life, and he accepted it. He said he's willing to take me however he can. He was disappointed that I won't marry again, but he said he he that he understood."

Maggie hugged Chelsea. "I'm happy for you, Chelsea. As long as you're happy that's really all that matters."

Chelsea got up from the table.

"I've got a lunch to prepare for us, and a bit of cleaning to do as well, but before we have our lunch-bunch meeting, I've got somewhere I want to go."

"Where?"

"The cemetery. I want to visit Carl and let him know that I'm going to Paris. I don't think he'll mind, do you?"

Maggie smiled, shook her head, and tried not to cry.

"I don't think he'll mind one bit."

As usual Maggie's lunch-bunch friends each looked beautiful on the computer monitor, and she told them so.

"I don't know what you ladies are doing, or if it's the Massachusetts cold winter that's giving you all your rosy cheeks, but you ladies look amazing."

Both Jane and Rachel joined the video with their cell phones. Everyone else sat in front of their computer. It wasn't the way they normally got together, but with everyone traveling and preparing for Christmas, it was impossible to get two or more together in one room.

Chelsea filled Maggie's wine glass with Pinot Grigio and teased their friends.

"You see the downside of us not being together? Two of us get to drink something awesome, the rest of you aren't so lucky."

Rachel fumbled with her cell phone, eventually securing it on her car's dashboard.

"Rachel, you must be freezing in your car. You didn't have to come online if it wasn't convenient. We all know how busy you are with your move to Cape Cod."

Rachel's voice broke up several times during the call.

"I'm fine, Maggie. I'm on my way to the house to check on the contractor. I've got a couple of water leaks because the roof needs to be replaced. I have to wait until spring to do the whole roof. For now, I'm just patching the trouble spots."

Chelsea took a sip of her wine, and then yelled into the monitor.

"Rachel,…"

Maggie stopped her.

"Chelsea, you don't have to yell. I know Rachel's miles away but trust me, yelling won't matter. She's not any farther than she was when she lived in Andover. You can just speak in your normal voice."

"Sorry, guys. I didn't mean to scream. Rachel, how's Everly?"

"She's wonderful. I'm in love of course. Everything she does I think no baby has ever done before and of course, she's a genius."

Kelly laughed. "I thought that too when I had my first baby. When the second one came, I changed my mind."

Chelsea decided to share her news with the group.

"Sebastian asked me to go to Paris with him. He's got a home there and plans to stay for about six months. I'm not staying that long, but I've agreed to go for maybe a month or so. I'm not sure. I'll know more when I get there."

Kelly, who traveled the world for her job, gave her opinion. "You're going to love it there. You'll have to let me know where you're staying. I might get a chance to fly over and meet up with you."

"That would be great. I'm trying to convince Maggie and Paolo to come in the new year. He said that he thinks they'd love it. I'm not sure if I can join the lunch-bunch January get together but if I can, I will."

Diana cut in. "I'm thinking of retiring from the bakery. I'm not sure what I want to do next, but I can't keep up this pace forever. It's exhausting."

Teasing, Maggie clapped her hands, "Let's all quit and follow Chelsea to Paris."

Everyone cheered and agreed it was a great idea, even if she was joking.

With Rachel and Jane's connections coming in and out, the group ended their video call early. Skipping their January meeting was a real possibility since several of the women couldn't guarantee attendance. They'd know better as the day drew near.

Maggie sat back in her chair and felt the pain of yet another of her traditions slipping away. Careful not to overthink things, she laughed at herself and tried not to see everything through the lens of loss. She missed her friends and thought that a future lunch-bunch trip to Paris was a great idea. She laughed when the image of her friend descending upon Sebastian Barlowe's Paris home formed in her mind but she loved Chelsea too much to ever put that kind of curse on her.

CHAPTER 5

*H*ad Lauren not locked herself out of the house, she might never have seen them. It took an additional thirty minutes to look for the spare key under the snow and another fifteen to go back inside, find her keys and leave Jeff a note.

The idea to surprise him and have lunch together seemed like a good one at the time. Now, staring at the paper, she felt sad for missing him, and angry for wasting valuable work time.

The drive back to her office didn't stop her from meeting her obligations. Placing a call to her office using the car's handsfree Bluetooth meant she could salvage at least part of her calendar to-do list.

"Nell, did you contact Mr. Foster like I asked you to?"

"Yes, I spoke with him and we're going to look at a few properties later this afternoon."

"Great. I don't want him to think that I'm dropping the ball on him. I've got too many…"

Minutes of silence followed, as Lauren passed Roman's Pub. Through the window she could see Jeff and a woman having drinks and talking.

"Lauren, are you still there?"

Startled, Lauren answered, "Yes. Yes, I'm here. I'll be in the office within thirty minutes. Let's talk then. I've got to go."

She ended the call without waiting for Nell to respond. Pulling her car into a parking spot on the side of the road.

Maybe I'm seeing things. It's probably someone who looks like Jeff.

Her heart racing, she walked down the sidewalk and closer to the Pub. Light snow started to fall even though the sun was out. A few flakes landed on her face and tears started to fill her eyes.

I can't cry here. I can't cry here.

She stared at the man in the window, watching him laugh at whatever the woman had said. He looked embarrassed as she pushed a few strands of his hair from his face—a gesture Lauren had done a thousand times before.

Looking away, she walked quickly to her car and got inside. Suddenly grateful for the keyless ignition, her shaking hands pressed the button, put the car in drive, and turned the wheel, driving out onto the road.

She wiped her eyes and willed them to focus. She needed to think, to plan, to understand what was happening. Whatever she had on her calendar for the rest of the day she'd cancel. If she was lucky, neither Nell nor Brian would notice anything wrong, but that seemed unlikely given the fact that things were far worse than just wrong. Her life had been suddenly turned upside down and everything she believed about her marriage had been ripped away from her with a single glance inside a restaurant window.

Lauren stared at the papers on her desk. two hours had passed since she saw Jeff with another woman. There was work to be done but she felt numb, frozen in her chair, unable to make sense of the listings in front of her.

She looked at the clock. By now, Jeff would be picking up the girls from school. What would he do before he got them? Would he fix his hair, or go back home and take a shower, removing any evidence of the other woman? Would his mind be on Olivia and Lily, or would he be thinking about his mistress and how they'd spent that morning doing who knows what?

Nell knocked on her office door.

"Callum Foster is here, so I'm going to take him to look at the properties we talked about."

Something inside Lauren stirred her into action.

"No. Let me take him. I'm sorry, I should have mentioned this before, but I need to talk to him about something."

It scared her how quickly and easily she could lie.

"I need to talk investments with him."

Surprised, Nell handed her paperwork to Lauren.

"Of course. No problem. I'll let him know that you'll be showing him the properties."

Lauren didn't look at Nell but instead just nodded. She felt like her brain had complete control over her actions and the out-of-body experience gave her the excuse she needed to justify her choice.

She grabbed her coat and tote bag along with the listings sheets and walked out to the front of the office. Extending her hand to Callum, she welcomed him.

"Hello, Callum. Can I get you anything. Water? Coffee?"

"No, thank you, I'm fine."

"Great. Let's take my car if you don't mind."

"Not at all."

Lauren looked at Nell. "Text me if you need me for anything."

Nell smiled. "Will do."

Callum wasn't dressed in his usual suit and tie, and instead wore jeans and a sweater over his shirt, a leather jacket completed the look which made Lauren feel overdressed.

"All but one of these properties are within forty minutes' drive from your work. One is a condo in the Back Bay of Boston which is perfect if you want to live in the city. I think it's important for you to have the option of city living as well."

"Sounds great."

They rode in silence for a few minutes before Callum spoke.

"I was pleasantly surprised to hear that you'd be the one taking me out."

The wording confused Lauren.

"Taking you out?"

"Yes, you know, showing me these properties. I was under the impression that you were avoiding me."

She tried to remain indifferent, as if none of this was a big deal.

"What would make you think that?"

"Well, we got on so well from the start, I was surprised when Nell told me that she'd be the one handling my interests."

Lauren shrugged. "I've just been very busy, that's all. I wanted to make sure that you got the attention that you needed. I wasn't certain I'd be able to do that with my workload."

"Forgive me for pushing this, but isn't the company yours?"

Lauren pulled up to the first property and turned off the car.

"Your point is?"

"My point is that you have complete control over the schedule. I think the reason you and I are in this car right now is perhaps because you wanted to see me again."

A mixture of embarrassment and anger colored Lauren's face. She didn't know what to say and blurted out the first thing that came into her head.

"Why do men cheat?"

The question took him aback and he shook his head in disbelief.

"What? Where did that come from? If you remember, I'm neither married nor dating anyone."

They sat in silence for a minute until the look on his face indicated that he understood her meaning.

"Oh, I see. I'm sorry. I didn't know."

Not wanting to divulge too much she diverted the conversation away from her and Jeff.

"I'm not sure you do. You see, my father cheated on my mother before he died. Several times, as it happens—pulled the rug right out from under her."

Callum guessed there was something more.

"And now, it's happened to you."

She played with her wedding band, twirling it around her finger.

"This morning. I just found out. I saw him with another woman."

He put his hand on her arm.

"I'm so sorry. I wish I had an answer for you as to why a man would cheat when he so obviously has a wonderful wife at home. I suppose it really has more to do with his needing a stranger to validate him in some way. I really don't know; I've never been in this sort of situation before."

"You've never cheated on anyone?"

Callum shook his head. "No. Never."

She realized that she could have talked to her sisters or her friends or even Nell back at the office about Jeff. Instead, she wanted to talk to Callum, and it had nothing to do with wanting a man's perspective. Fully aware that from their first encounter Callum was flirting with her, Lauren's first instinct was to hurt Jeff in some way.

Callum wanted to be with her, and Lauren took that reality and used it to get back at her husband. It was silly, really. It wasn't like Jeff would ever know about it, but it didn't matter. She needed to lash out in some way, and this was the only weapon at her disposal.

However, the minute she'd taken such a reckless action, she regretted it. Spending time with Callum Foster wouldn't solve a thing. Knowing nothing would happen between them, she felt ashamed that she'd had so little respect for Callum to use him this way.

What's wrong with you? He thinks you're such a wonderful wife. He doesn't even know you. He doesn't have a clue who you are, and by the looks of things, neither do you.

"I'm sorry for spending our time on my marital problems instead of focusing on these properties. How about we forget all this and go inside and check out the house?"

"Lauren, I think you know that I'd love nothing more than to spend time with you outside of this real estate business. I know you're going through a difficult time right now. It would be inappropriate for me to do anything more than be a shoulder to cry on if you need it. But know that if you're ever ready for more, I'll be waiting."

Lauren smiled and thanked him, but she also knew that she'd never take him up on his offer. There was only one thing she wanted to do—what she needed to do—and Callum Foster didn't factor into her plans at all.

CHAPTER 6

*M*aggie watched as Paolo and Trevor pulled several strands of Christmas lights from the large box. She'd stayed clear of any involvement in the decorating process, even letting her husband and son-in-law buy the inn's Christmas tree from Murphy's Holiday lot. Nothing about the island could convince anyone that they were shopping in a winter wonderland, but Murphy Jenkins, or Murph, as everyone called him did his best to turn his parking lot into a Florida version of the North Pole.

The large tree sat in the front room of the inn so that anyone passing would be able to see it from the driveway. Byron's admonishing her for having little holiday spirit reminded her that no matter what she was feeling inside, she'd need to pretend for her guests at the very least.

She could see that Trevor was losing his patience with Paolo and thought that just this once she better get involved.

"What's the problem?"

"It would have made sense if your husband put these lights away last year in a more organized fashion. We're going to be here for hours untangling these things before we ever get them up on the house. I'm at the point where I'm ready to drive to Target and buy all new lights."

Paolo shook his head. "Why in the world would we spend money on new lights when we have perfectly good ones here?"

Her hands on her hips, Maggie hated to ask the obvious, but did so anyway.

"Have either of you thought to plug the lights in to see if they work first?"

Paolo and Trevor froze in place, each looking at the other. Trevor spoke first.

"Paolo, I thought you already tested them."

"Not me. I thought you did."

"Why would I do it when I thought you already checked?"

Rather than listen to this endless go 'round, Maggie marched over to them and found the plug for each strand. One by one she plugged the lights into the socket and only one strand lit up. Frustrated, she turned to Trevor.

"I think your instinct to buy new ones is a good idea. Why don't you two drive over to Target? Get all new lights. No point in trusting this single strand to work. It's as old as the rest."

Paolo interrupted. "I'll drive."

Trevor shook his head.

"No. I'll drive. My truck is already facing forward. I'll drive."

"Your truck is too big to take to Target. We're not buying construction materials. Let's just take the SUV."

"Paolo, I'm perfectly capable…"

Maggie couldn't stand it anymore.

"STOP! Who cares what car you take. The two of you get in Trevor's truck and go."

Maggie looked at her husband who understood her lack of patience with them and didn't argue.

As they walked toward the back door, she cautioned them. "If the two of you can't stop squabbling, I'm going to have to hire someone to put the lights up, so you better figure out how to get along."

It was bad enough that Maggie already felt miserable about the holiday, the last thing she needed was dealing with two childish adults. She walked back into the front room and ran her hands over the Christmas ornaments. Lifting one that Sarah had made when she was a little girl. Her fingers twirled it around watching the red and gold globe sparkle. Pieces captured the sun and bounced the reflecting light onto the wall.

Dropping it back into the box, she looked inside and remembered the history of each ornament. Some were bought, others handmade, they represented years of holiday memories, and it pained her to think that might be all she'd have this Christmas. She'd have to be content with the memories of past holidays and try her best to build new ones with Paolo.

Looking around the room she felt angry. She'd worked so hard to find her place in the world, but the cost of her new life seemed unfair to her somehow.

What did you expect? Did you think your children would drop everything and follow you to Captiva whenever you called? You wanted them to live their best life and now you want them to take care of you instead? What kind of mother does that?

Feeling selfish and ashamed, she started to cry. How did this happen? Captiva was Paradise to her, and one doesn't cry in Paradise.

"Mom? Where are you?"

Maggie sat up and wiped the tears from her cheeks.

"Sarah? I'm in the front room."

Noah ran into the room ahead of Sarah and Sophia.

"Grandma!"

"Hey, you guys. I'm glad you stopped by. Maybe you can help decorate the Christmas tree when Paolo and Trevor get back."

"Where did they go?"

"Target. I sent them to get new Christmas lights. Looks like the ones we have aren't working. Would you all like something to eat? I was going to prepare a lunch for us anyway."

"That sounds great. I thought the kids would like to see your tree but somehow I imagined it decorated already."

Once again, Maggie felt the sting of disapproval.

"I know. I'm failing Christmas. So, sue me."

"Whoa. Why so defensive?"

"I'm sorry. I guess I'm just not feeling very Christmassy."

"Said no innkeeper ever. I thought of all people you'd be in your usual holiday spirit. If I remember correctly, aren't you the Christmas in July type? Growing up I think you loved the holiday more than us kids."

Maggie shrugged. "I'm sure the closer to Christmas we get, the more excited I'll be."

Maggie didn't realize Noah was listening.

"Grandma, don't you like Santa?"

"Oh, Noah. I do. I love Santa. I'm just a little tired today. I bet Sophia will love Santa too. You've both been very good this year so I'm sure you'll get lots of presents under the tree."

Trevor and Paolo came into the room and Noah ran to his father.

"Daddy! Mommy said we should help you with the decorations."

"She did? Your mommy is pretty smart because Grandpa Paolo and I sure do need the help."

Maggie got up from her chair and started for the kitchen.

"You all enjoy decorating while I go make us a nice lunch."

"Mom, can you please put Sophia's bottle in the refrigerator?"

"Sure."

Maggie took the bottle from Sarah and walked to the kitchen. Looking at her family hovered around boxes of ornaments and all talking at once, she smiled, grateful for each one. To complain about anything in her life felt wrong, and so, she promised herself that she'd focus on the good and let go of what she couldn't control.

Chelsea finished her lunch and carried the dishes to the sink. After cleaning up, she walked to the lanai and looked at her canvas. Today was the first time in weeks that she wasn't in the mood to paint. She attributed it to the new changes in her life.

Paris. Carl and I always said we'd go to Paris.

She went back inside and climbed the stairs to her bedroom. Her closet was stuffed with so many clothes, shoes, and handbags that she had a hard time reaching the top shelf. On the tips of her toes, she pushed against the hanging garments and leaned on them for support.

Once she found the right box, she pulled it down and placed it on the bed. Sitting beside it, she opened the box and gingerly took out a card with a single paper folded inside. A pressed flower fell onto her lap, and she carefully returned it to the card, pressing the pages to secure it once again. She opened the paper and read the letter.

To my girl.

I hope you don't mind my calling you that. You'll always be my girl. When you need a pick-me-up, come back and read my words once again. I'm always going to be with you, no matter whatever happens in the future, you can count on it. Close your eyes and remember my face. Can you see the way I'm looking at you? That's love sweetheart. I'll always love you no matter where I am...in this world and the next, we will never part.

. . .

I need you to do something for me. Promise me that you'll be happy. I won't rest until I know that you are living your best life. Death isn't the end. We'll see each other again, I promise you. Until then, have fun, travel, eat great food and look for me wherever you go.

I'm sorry we never got to Paris. I know how much you wanted to see the Eiffel Tower. Go to Paris as soon as you can. Go up to the top of the tower and look down at the beautiful Parisian landscape. Now, close your eyes again. Can you see me there? I'm right next to you. We've reached the top together, and isn't it marvelous?

Carl

Chelsea didn't want to cry. She'd done plenty of that since Carl's death. Reading his words once again was an exercise in morale boosting. She needed to hear his voice in her head. She imagined him in the room with her, telling her how to live, how to put one foot in front of the other until she could fly.

She didn't need to look at this card to remember their love, but to strengthen it. Living was difficult without him, but she would continue to do her best until her last breath. If that meant going to Paris with Sebastian then so be it. Carl would never begrudge her that.

CHAPTER 7

For the last two years Maggie had booked guests into the Key Lime Garden Inn during the Christmas holiday season. She badly wanted to establish the inn and she'd sacrificed being with her family during that time because of it. This year was different. She'd hoped to have her family with her, but instead, she begrudgingly booked every room and decided to make the best of her situation.

Paolo had sensed Maggie's disappointment.

"You do realize that you could close the inn and we could travel to Boston to be with the kids. If being with them during the holiday means so much to you, I'm fine with it."

"You are the sweetest husband. Thank you for saying that but no, that wouldn't work either. I'd miss Sarah and her family if we went up there. I wanted all my children with me this year, and since that can't happen, I'm just going to have to accept it and move on."

Standing on the stepladder so that she could place the Christmas star on the top of the tree, she pretended to be content.

ANNIE CABOT

"I'm looking forward to meeting new people and baking Christmas cookies. It will be fun."

She knew that she wasn't fooling anyone, least of all her husband who knew how upset she really was. At least with the inn fully booked there would be lots of activity around the place. She took comfort in knowing that she'd get to watch Noah and Sophia open their Christmas presents. Maggie vowed to stay upbeat and positive during the next two weeks even if it killed her.

She was surprised when she heard the front door bells jingle. The guest rooms were already full, and she wasn't expecting anyone.

"Hi, Mom."

Paolo put his paper down and Maggie got down from the stepladder.

Lauren stood in the foyer with Olivia and Lily on either side of her two luggage bags.

Her grandchildren ran to her and wrapped their arms around her waist. Maggie bent down and hugged Olivia and Lily and then instructed them to follow Paolo into the kitchen to get some brownies and milk. She then turned to look at Lauren. Knowing something was terribly wrong she waited for her daughter to say something. When Lauren did speak, Maggie was shocked.

"I've left Jeff."

Maggie could tell that Lauren had put on a brave face for the sake of the girls, but now she looked like she was about to melt down before Maggie's eyes. She hugged Lauren and then walked to the kitchen door.

"Paolo, Lauren and I are going over to the carriage house. Keep Olivia and Lily with you, all right?"

Paolo waved back as Maggie grabbed the luggage. The two women walked to the carriage house with Lauren fighting back tears. Once inside, Lauren fell face down onto Maggie's bed and cried uncontrollably.

Maggie ran to Lauren and leaned down trying to console her as best she could. She handed her a box of tissues and waited, letting her cry as long as she needed before asking any questions.

"Tell me what happened. I thought you and Jeff were working with a marriage counselor."

Lauren sat up and took her coat off.

"We were, but a marriage counselor isn't going to fix this. Jeff's been seeing another woman."

Maggie couldn't believe it. Her first instinct was to get Jeff on the phone and give him a piece of her mind. As angry as she was, Maggie thought it best to stay calm and try to help her daughter find a way through this mess. She grabbed a box of tissues and handed it to Lauren.

"What did he say?"

"What do you mean?"

"I mean, how did he explain himself? Where did he meet her?"

Lauren shook her head, "I don't know who she is. I didn't talk to him about it."

"What are you talking about? Didn't he tell you that there was someone else? How did you find out?"

"I saw him. I was on my way to the office, and I drove by this restaurant and saw him having lunch with her. It was obvious they were more than friends. I could tell."

"Whoa, Lauren, hang on. You have no idea who this woman is or why she and Jeff were having lunch. Don't you think there's a possibility that you're over-reacting to this? It might be nothing."

Lauren abruptly got up from the bed.

"How can you say that after what Dad did?"

Lauren's reaction shocked Maggie.

"Wait one minute, young lady. Don't you dare compare your marriage to mine. I understand that you're upset, but you don't have all the details and therefore don't have the right to pass judgment on anything. Whatever is going on with Jeff, you

ANNIE CABOT

should have talked to him before assuming things. Jeff isn't your father, and I'm not you."

Defeated, Lauren sat back onto the bed, and looked at Maggie.

"I'm sorry, Mom. I didn't mean what I said."

Maggie felt for Lauren, but her daughter needed to hear the truth.

"Lauren, as much as I love having you here, you never should have come without first talking to Jeff. What did he say when you told him you were coming?"

"I told him that we were going to spend Christmas with you."

"He didn't think that was strange?"

"He did, but instead of asking me to stay and have Christmas with him, all he said was it was stupid to take the girls out of school so early. Other than that, he didn't put up too much of a fuss. Imagine that? Of course, I already knew the reason. With the girls and me gone that gives him all the time in the world to be with his mistress."

Maggie didn't know what to do. The fact that Daniel had several affairs didn't make her an expert on such things, and it was a mistake for Lauren to think otherwise. The real truth was that it meant that Maggie could understand the pain and confusion that her daughter was feeling. The worst part was that there was very little she could do to alleviate that pain. The best Maggie could offer was a place to stay, along with her love and support until Lauren and Jeff decided on next steps.

"Oh, my goodness, I forgot. All the rooms at the inn are full of guests. I didn't think we'd have any family visiting, so we accepted reservations right up until December twenty-third."

"Don't worry, Mom. I'm sure we can stay at a hotel nearby. Why don't we see what's available."

"No way. You have to stay here. Let me talk to Paolo and we'll figure something out. You and the girls are going to need our support and I hate the thought that you'd be in a hotel. In the meantime, why don't you come back downstairs to the kitchen, and I'll get Riley to make us all a nice lunch."

Lauren smiled and hugged Maggie. "I'm surprised you aren't offering me a cup of tea. That's your usual answer for everything."

"Who says I'm not offering tea? I'm making a pot as soon as we get into the kitchen."

Sarah helped set the tables in a horseshoe shape, leaving enough room for people to walk by the displays of Christmas items. Additional tables for the silent auction were placed at the far end of the room. Local businesses had donated several coveted items including a sunset cruise run by Powell Water Sports.

The first annual benefit for the Outreach Center's Battered Women Shelter had so much support from the community that Sarah was confident it would be a great success. Originally, she wanted the benefit to take place on Captiva Island, but it wasn't a practical choice. The location was difficult to get to, and those who the benefit would help most lived off-island.

Ciara carried trays of soda, chips and dip and Bill Crandall followed behind with a crock pot filled with Swedish meatballs. Several women were in the kitchen proving there was no such thing as too many cooks in the kitchen. There would be plenty of food along with a table filled with baked items for sale.

Bill plugged the crock pot in and then looked around the room. "Sarah, do you need me to do anything else?"

"The only thing left is helping Ed with the chairs. I think he's in the back storage room. Thanks, Bill."

Only a few more hours and the room would be filled with holiday shoppers and Christmas cheer. Sarah connected her cell phone Bluetooth to the Bose speakers and found her Christmas playlist. A text came through from her mother interrupting her focus.

Please call me as soon as you can.

It wasn't like her mother to send such an urgent text, so Sarah called Maggie right away.

"Mom, what is it?"

Her mother whispering, Sarah could barely hear her.

"Lauren's here. She left Jeff."

"What? Mom, I can't hear you. What did you say?"

The second time, the words came through loud and clear.

"Lauren left Jeff. She's here with Olivia and Lily. The girls don't know anything more than they're here to celebrate Christmas with me and Paolo. You've got to get over here. Lauren's going to need all our support."

"Mom, I can't leave. I'm in the middle of getting ready for the benefit. It starts in two hours. I guess I could drive over after, but it will be late."

There was a pause on the other end of the line.

"Mom? Are you still there?"

"I'm here. On second thought, don't come tonight. Tomorrow makes more sense. Lauren and the girls can stay here in the carriage house, but all the rooms are booked until Christmas, so I don't have room for them. Any chance you guys could take them in?"

Sarah wanted to help. Although she and Trevor had just put an addition on their house, she worried that it might be cramped. Still, there would be more room than what the carriage house could provide. She knew her mother well enough to know that a hotel would be out of the question, considering the seriousness of the situation.

"I guess we can try. Let me talk to Trevor and see what we can do."

"Thanks, Sarah. I'm sorry Paolo and I won't be at the benefit, but I think it's best we stay here for Lauren and the girls."

"Of course, don't give it another thought, and Mom, try not to worry. I'm sure that Lauren and Jeff will work this out, whatever the problem is, I know they love each other. There's no way they're going to throw all these years away. I'm sure of it."

The truth was that Sarah wasn't sure of anything. She could see the tension between Lauren and Jeff at her wedding, but she'd hoped by now things would be better. Her mother's sadness over not being with her children this holiday season was bad enough, now, with Lauren's latest drama, their Christmas was about to get much worse.

CHAPTER 8

Chelsea appeared at the back door of the inn, looking for Maggie but she was nowhere to be found. Riley and Grace were in the kitchen and except for the ever-full pot of coffee, it didn't look like there was much chance of her getting something to eat.

Unusual as it was for Maggie not to be in the kitchen, Chelsea came inside and poured herself a cup of coffee.

"Would you care for an omelet, Chelsea?"

"No thank you, Riley. The coffee will do. Is Maggie around?"

Grace shook her head. "I haven't seen her this morning. Paolo is in the garden already. Maybe he knows where she is."

"Thanks."

Chelsea carried her coffee cup outside. She waved to Paolo who was at the far end of the garden.

"Good morning, Chelsea. I assume you're looking for Maggie. She's upstairs in the carriage house with Lauren, Olivia, and Lily."

"What? I didn't know they were coming down."

"They weren't. Long story that I'm sure Maggie will share with you. Why don't you send her a text and let her know you're here. I'd tell you to go upstairs but the truth is there's a bit of drama going on."

Chelsea laughed. "I guess that explains why you're in the garden this early."

Paolo smiled and nodded. "You've found me out."

Chelsea didn't have to text as Maggie called from the window. "Chelsea, come on up."

Lauren and the girls were still in their pajamas and Maggie was getting changed.

"This is a pleasant surprise. When did you all get here?"

Lauren and the girls took turns hugging Chelsea.

"They got here yesterday afternoon."

"I didn't know you guys were coming."

Maggie laughed. "Neither did I. Unfortunately, all the rooms are booked, so we all camped in here last night."

"Mom won't let us stay at a hotel which is ridiculous. There are plenty of Bed & Breakfasts on the island. We can just go to one of them and still be close."

Chelsea knew Maggie well enough that she wasn't surprised by this at all.

"No need to look for a B&B. You all can stay at my place. I've got plenty of room."

Maggie clapped her hands. "Oh, Chelsea, are you sure? That could solve the problem. This way Lauren and the girls will be close by and won't have to pay big bucks to stay at a hotel."

Lauren wasn't so sure. "Chelsea I know you. You'll be running around cooking for us and making a fuss. I don't want you to go to any trouble."

"Don't be silly. It's no trouble at all. Honestly, I'd love the company."

Even Olivia seemed excited about the possibility of staying at Chelsea's house.

"Can we, Mommy? Please?"

With so many in her corner, Chelsea knew it wouldn't take much to get Lauren to agree.

"Ok. If you promise not to wait on us all the time, we'd love to stay with you."

Chelsea didn't want to admit it, but without family, it was hard for her to have a reason to celebrate the holiday. Now, with Lauren and the girls staying with her, she'd have family to share Christmas with. If they stayed long enough, she might even get a visit from Santa for the first time in many years.

The next morning, Sarah asked Trevor to watch Noah and Sophia while she visited her mother and Lauren. Trevor agreed that although it would be tight, they'd make room for Lauren and the girls. Sarah wanted to get over to Captiva to let her mother know so Maggie could stop worrying.

When she arrived at the inn, Lauren, Lily and Olivia had already gone to Chelsea's house. Her mother rocked back and forth on the porch swing deep in thought. Sarah hugged her mother and sat next to her.

"I'm glad they'll be with Chelsea. I think that's an arrangement that will work for everyone. Tell me what happened. It must have been pretty bad for Lauren to come all the way to Florida."

Her mother could barely get the words out.

"Apparently Jeff is having an affair."

Sarah was shocked. "Get out! That's impossible. He's crazy about Lauren. I've never seen two people more in love or perfect for each other. Why in the world would he do this? What did he have to say for himself?"

Maggie put her hands to her face and lowered her head.

"That's just it, Sarah. He never got a chance to say anything. She saw him sitting in a restaurant with another woman and the impression she got was that they were more than friends."

"That's it? She didn't confront him?"

"Apparently not."

Sarah sat back against the swing and sighed.

"Well, this is a pickle."

Maggie looked at Sarah and laughed. "A pickle?"

Sarah smiled. "I picked it up from my son. Noah says it all the time, and I have no idea where he heard it."

Maggie sat up straight and then leaned against Sarah.

"I like it. You're absolutely right. This certainly is a pickle."

Olivia and Lily explored every room in Chelsea's house. Finally deciding which room should be theirs, they bounced on a queen-sized bed in one of the guest rooms.

"Girls, stop that. This isn't our house and you don't want to break Chelsea's bed. Not to mention, I don't want to find myself at the hospital because you fell and hit your head."

The girls stopped bouncing and sat politely on the edge of the bed. Chelsea did her best to cheer them up.

"How about you two come downstairs and help me find something good to watch on tv?"

They quickly ran to the stairs and followed Chelsea to the living room. As soon as they found a television show both girls could agree on, Chelsea brought them milk and cookies and placed everything on the coffee table.

"I'll be right back, I'm going to help your mom unpack, but we can hear you so call if you need something. Ok?"

The girls nodded without taking their eyes off the tv.

Chelsea found Lauren in her room sitting on the side of the bed staring out the window.

"How are you doing? Do you need any help getting settled in?"

"No. Thank you, Chelsea. I'm almost done."

Chelsea wanted to help but didn't know what to say. As yet, no one had shared a thing with her. Something terrible had happened and if she had to guess, it was trouble in Lauren and Jeff's marriage.

"Lauren, I'm not sure what's happened, but I'm here if you need to talk."

Lauren smiled at her, and patted the bed.

"You might as well have a seat and let me explain. You and I both know that my mother is only hours away from bringing you up to speed on everything."

Chelsea sat and laughed at that. "You know your mother pretty well."

"I do indeed, besides, you're family, and heaven knows I could use as much advice as I can get."

They stayed on the bed talking for two hours, checking on Olivia and Lily occasionally. Chelsea let Lauren cry and talk through her frustration over the months of counseling and therapy that had led nowhere. She talked about her work and the joy she got from building her career. She also shared her love for Jeff and her desire to fix whatever was wrong with their marriage. But, that was before she saw him with another woman.

"Lauren, you're never going to fix things with Jeff if you don't talk to him. Running away won't solve a thing."

Lauren got up off the bed and looked in the mirror. Her makeup no longer on her face, but in the tissues she held in her hands. She brushed her hair and tried to keep her voice from cracking, and she didn't want to cry again.

"I know you're right, but I just couldn't face him. I couldn't bring myself to talk about it."

"Why not? What are you afraid of?"

Lauren turned and looked at her.

"I was afraid he was going to do to me what Dad did to Mom. I didn't want to hear that he was in love with someone else and that he wanted a divorce."

Chelsea finally understood why Lauren came to Captiva. Staying in Florida would keep everything intact, at least through Christmas. Lauren couldn't allow her world to fall apart, not now. Maybe in the new year, when she was ready and strong enough to hear him speak, but not until then.

It wasn't just Lauren's life that would be turned upside down. She had to think about Olivia and Lily as well. The pain she'd suffered due to her parents' divorce and her father's death, was an adult's struggle. What her girls would go through, Chelsea couldn't imagine.

If Lauren was unwilling to say all this to her mother, Chelsea would have to. By now, she was certain that Maggie was beside herself with worry. Confused and unable to help her daughter, she'd be hurting. Her best friend might be upset that Lauren felt more comfortable talking to Chelsea about her fears than her own mother, but she'd have to push that thought aside, and talk to Maggie, and soon.

She wasn't naive. Chelsea knew there was a very good chance that Lauren would experience the same fate as her mother. There was nothing Chelsea could do about that except, along with the rest of the Wheeler family, be as supportive as possible. The rest would be up to Jeff and Lauren.

CHAPTER 9

*T*he first time Maggie called a "Code Red" was when Beth was in high school and wouldn't talk to her for two weeks. They hadn't quarreled and there was no major event that Maggie could attribute to Beth's silence. She had no other choice but to, as Maggie liked to call it, "Bring in the Troops" to solve the mystery.

The support of Beth's siblings in a difficult time made all the difference and, even though Maggie never did find out what the problem was, she had every confidence in her children to help Beth through whatever was troubling her.

Over the years, everyone in the family used the alarm signal during times of crisis. This time, Maggie didn't have the power to alleviate Lauren's distress, but she could find a way to get the Christmas she'd been hoping for. What words she would use to justify the Code Red phone calls she hadn't figured out just yet.

She didn't use it when Christopher came to live with her on Captiva during his recovery, and if ever a Code Red was needed, it was then. His particular trauma was best handled one family member at a time. On any given day it was impossible to know exactly how to deal with Christopher. In the end, doing without the Code Red made the most sense.

Maggie wondered what she could say to convince her children that Lauren's situation was dire, and they all needed to get to Captiva as soon as possible to support their sister in her time of need.

The idea was sneaky, but she was desperate. As always, she'd need to talk to Chelsea about her plan because her partner in crime knew how to balance Maggie's crazy ideas with a touch of reality. Chelsea's usual ride or die attitude would come in handy, and Maggie couldn't wait to run the idea by her best friend.

As luck would have it, Chelsea appeared at the back door just before dinner.

"Hey, I'm not used to seeing you standing there this time of day. Is your clock not working?"

"Very funny. To hear you tell it, I only show up in this kitchen to eat your scones and drink your coffee."

Maggie laughed. "Well?"

Chelsea shrugged, "You might be right."

Chelsea walked to the door leading to the dining room.

"Looks like you've got a full house for dinner tonight. Maybe we should talk tomorrow morning. I can get here early."

"No. It's fine. I just came over to get a bottle of white wine out of the refrigerator. Riley and Grace have everything under control. Do you want to come up to the carriage house?"

"If you're drinking wine, you're not doing it alone. I have to assume this is for you and Paolo. I don't want to interrupt. Let's talk in the morning."

"Paolo is still at Sanibellia and will be for at least another hour. This is for later."

As they walked across the driveway, Maggie thought of Lauren and wondered if Chelsea wanted to talk without Lauren hearing her.

"Is everything all right at your house? The girls settling in? I hope this isn't a problem for you."

"No, not at all. I'm happy to have them. I wanted to talk to you about a conversation I had with Lauren. I think you need to hear this because it might help you to understand what's on her mind."

"On second thought, there were two bottles of this wine in the fridge, I'll get another one for Paolo and me. I think you and I should start on this one."

Maggie selected two glasses from her cabinet and opened the bottle. She filled the two glasses halfway and carried them into the living room. Handing Chelsea hers, she took a deep breath, not sure she wanted to hear what Chelsea had to say.

Chelsea sat on the sofa and took a sip of her wine.

"Bottom line is Lauren is terrified that Jeff is going to do to her exactly what Daniel did to you. She basically ran away from home just to avoid him telling her that he's in love with someone else and wants a divorce."

Maggie sighed, "I thought something like that was going on."

"You did?"

"Chelsea, how could I not? Except for the part of Daniel dying, it's starting to look like Daniel and me all over again."

"She's afraid to say this to you. I think she's worried you'll feel responsible in some way."

"That's crazy."

"Of course it is, but to Lauren, it isn't. I think she feels like she's genetically predisposed to having a cheating husband."

"First of all, none of us knows for certain that Jeff cheated. I know what she saw looked incriminating but it's still not fact until she confronts him with all this. The guy is innocent until proven guilty, and the only way she's going to know for sure is if she talks to him."

"Which she refuses to do."

Maggie rolled her eyes and took a gulp of her wine. Her Code Red plan was starting to look better with every minute that passed. Lauren was being stubborn, and no amount of talking to her was going to change anything. Maggie needed to get her children on board, and fast.

Although no one else was in the room, Maggie sat close to Chelsea and began sharing her plan in hushed tones.

"I have an idea."

When Maggie finished explaining the details of Code Red she sat back on the sofa and waited for Chelsea's reaction.

"Let me get this straight. Your children have other plans for Christmas, and you want to disrupt their lives with a crisis that you, Lauren and I are perfectly capable of handling ourselves? Do I have that right?"

Her plan sounded better when she formed it.

"When you say it like that, it makes me sound awful."

Chelsea poured more wine into her glass.

"How would you say it then?"

Maggie sat up straight and convinced herself that she was doing something noble and necessary.

"You don't understand Chelsea. The Wheeler Family Code Red alert is very sacred. I'm sure when they all get here, they'll see the value in it. Either that, or none of my kids will ever speak to me again."

The first person Maggie called was Michael. It was a strategic move and one that had the greatest chance for success. Michael hadn't completely ruled out traveling to Captiva for Christmas, but his wife, Brea, would have the final say.

Maggie explained the situation to him and paused to hear his reaction.

"Oh, man, that's awful. I knew they were having problems, but I never expected this from Jeff."

"Well, Michael we can't be sure of anything just yet. I think this will be a terrible Christmas for Lauren, Olivia, and Lily without Jeff. You and I know how much strength she gets from the support of family. I wish we could all be together to help her. I have no choice, I've got to call a Code Red, Michael. This is serious. I think it's up to her family to get her and the girls through whatever comes next. The most important thing is that all my grandchildren see lots of presents under the tree this year, especially Olivia and Lily."

The silence on the other end of the line meant that Michael didn't dismiss the idea.

"I'll have to talk to Brea. We were going to stay home this year, but Lauren and the girls need our support. I feel like going over to the house and confronting Jeff."

"No. Michael don't do that. We don't have all the facts and I think it would be a mistake for us to intervene before Lauren talks to him."

"You're right. Let me talk to Brea. Have you called anyone else?"

"No, not yet. I was going to call Christopher next. Unless you'd be willing to call him and Becca."

"No problem, Mom. Let me handle it. I can talk to Chris, and Beth as well. Don't worry about a thing. I'll talk to both of them. I'm sure we can make it happen. Although, we're running out of time. Do you think we'll be able to get flights down? We'll need eight seats. It's pretty last minute and it is Christmas after all."

Maggie had worried about the same thing. "Fingers crossed on that. Check with everyone and get back to me as soon as you can, and Michael, don't forget. Tell everyone I'm calling a Code Red. That should convince them of the seriousness of the situation."

"I will, Mom. Talk soon. Love you."

"Love you too, sweetie."

Maggie ended the call and finished the last of the wine. Paolo finally came home around nine o'clock and she was too exhausted from the day's events to do much more than fall into bed. For the first time in weeks, she had a glimmer of hope.

She lay on the bed looking at the moon through the window. There would be much to plan if all of her family was coming for Christmas. Suddenly panicked, she sat up in bed and put her head in her hands. She'd forgotten about the guests she had booked. Every room would be filled right up to December 23rd. What were the chances that Michael would be able to find available seats so close to Christmas?

Paolo sat up and put his arm around Maggie.

"What is it, honey? Are you all right?"

Maggie looked at Paolo and shook her head.

"I think I've done an impossible thing, and now I've got to make it possible."

"That sounds ominous. What impossible thing did you do?"

"I'm not sure just yet. Michael will call me tomorrow to confirm, but I might have convinced all the kids to be here for Christmas, and that's only ten days away. Do you think we can pull it off?"

Paolo kissed her temple and squeezed her tight.

"My love, if anyone can make the impossible, possible, it's you."

CHAPTER 10

*S*arah rummaged through the papers on her desk and then picked up the phone to call Ciara.

"Hey, Ciara, do you have a minute to talk?"

"Sure. What's up?"

"Do you mind coming down to my office instead of talking on the phone?"

"No problem. Do you want a coffee? I was just about to make one of my own."

"No, thanks, I've just made a cup of tea."

Ciara laughed. "Uh-oh, tea? This must be bad news."

Sarah smiled and couldn't get over how much of her mother she'd carried out into the world. Her mother's answer for any problem was a cup of tea, and now Sarah was doing the same thing and becoming infamous for it.

A few minutes later, Ciara appeared in her office. Sarah was going over the details of the domestic violence women's shelter benefit and felt proud that she'd run a successful event.

"Hey, your desk looks almost as bad as mine."

"I've still got a few hours left to go through this mess; hopefully I can get it all done before I leave today."

"So, what's going on that you needed to talk in person?"

"It's about Hope McKenna."

"What about her?"

"She's gone back with her husband."

Ciara put her head in her hands. "How did he get to her?"

Sarah sighed, "I'm not entirely sure. I thought I'd check with you to see if you've seen anything going on with her lately. I thought she was making really good progress, but now with this, I don't know."

"It's a setback for sure. I haven't seen a thing. She's been meeting with her therapist regularly. I think it's been going well. Have you tried to call her?"

Sarah nodded. "I did. No answer. It just goes to voicemail."

"You didn't leave your real name did you?"

"No, of course not. I know the protocol. I didn't leave a message at all. I'm beside myself with worry."

Sarah had a thought but was certain Ciara would disagree with her idea.

"I want to go over there."

"Over where?"

"To their house."

"Are you crazy? You know that might put her at risk, not to mention you and your pregnancy."

"I know, I get it, but hear me out. All I want to do is drive nearby. I won't go anywhere near the house. I just want to…"

"Stake out the place, that's what you're saying. What happens if you see him beating on her? Are you able to stay in the car and call the cops? Because I've got to say that if it were me, I'd have a hard time not jumping out and going after him. I think this is a bad idea."

Sarah looked at Ciara with a sheepish grin. "Not if you go with me."

Ciara got up from her chair and started pacing the room. She took a sip of her coffee and looked at Sarah.

"Now I know why you wouldn't talk on the phone. You knew I'd say no and hang up on you."

Sarah held her tongue and let Ciara work through the risk assessment as she watched.

"Just because there'd be two of us still doesn't mean we'll be able to keep our cool. One time I saw a woman getting beaten by her boyfriend and I jumped out of my car and ran toward them. The coward took off. That doesn't mean I couldn't have gotten myself killed. And it also doesn't mean that the guy didn't come back later and beat her again."

"Listen, I know what you're saying, but this might be a chance to put him away for a little bit while we get her back into the shelter."

"Right, because that worked so well before. There's a chance that we call the cops, they come, and she doesn't press charges, just like before. The guy never goes to jail."

"They'd have to take him away if they see him in the act, right?"

"Yeah. Probably, but that's a slim chance. If she presses charges, well, then that's a different thing altogether. The question is, will she?"

Sarah looked down at the papers on her desk. Her voice soft, she said, "I just want to get her back here. I don't know how else to do it, but I need to talk to her—convince her to come back. If she's alone, we could get her in the car and drive somewhere to talk just in case he comes home."

"You can't kidnap the woman."

"I know that silly. I'm just saying we drive somewhere away from the house. We can talk in the parking lot of the supermarket, and she can walk back with groceries. That way, if she won't come back to the shelter, at least he won't suspect anything."

Ciara sat back in her chair and looked directly into Sarah's eyes.

"You've been watching way too many police procedural television shows. If we're lucky...and that's a big if...we might pull this off without making things worse."

"Does that mean you'll do it?"

Ciara walked to the door. Well, if you're coming, let's go. I don't know how I let you talk me into these things. I've got to get another coffee before we leave."

"Thank you, Ciara."

"Uh-huh.

Sarah had no idea how long they'd be sitting in her car, but she was glad for the granola bar in her purse. She filled her to-go cup with more hot water, added another tea bag and a splash of almond milk. Looking at her desk she accepted the fact that the paperwork would have to wait. Saving Hope's life was more important than anything on her to-do list. She took a minute to say a quick prayer that all would go as planned and that Willy McKenna would never get another opportunity to harm his wife ever again.

The neighborhood streets were filled with children playing. No matter what was happening in the McKenna home, Sarah didn't think it would be exposed in the light of day. With too many witnesses around, Willy McKenna would most likely add new bruises to Hope's body where no one could see them, and he'd do it inside the house.

That was his way, and it wasn't unlike every other abusive relationship that Sarah had witnessed over these last months. Domestic violence was an epidemic, and she figured to save one life was one of the most important things she would ever do.

She had little qualification to handle the psychological effects of such trauma but felt that providing a safe place for women and their children was equally important. The women who came into the shelter were almost always drawn to share their stories with

Sarah. Trevor told her that she was an empath, and as such, unable to walk away when anyone she cared about was in distress.

Sarah was a perfect match for her job, but the nature of it meant she couldn't leave her work at the office. Countless hours thinking about how she could better serve the women and children in her community made Trevor concerned for her health and that of their unborn child.

Sarah pointed to the driveway.

"He's home, that's for sure. That's his truck."

Ciara had parked her car at the far end of the road and across the street. She'd been smart enough to bring binoculars with her but had to be careful. With so many people around, they'd bring attention to the car if anyone saw them peering through them to spy on the McKenna house.

Hope came out of the house briefly to put something in the trash barrel. Her husband followed her outside and was yelling at her. Sarah couldn't make out what he was saying, but it was obvious he was angry about something. Hope's face looked red and swollen.

Hope ran back inside the house and Willy chased after her. With the windows of the car lowered, Ciara and Sarah could hear the yelling but couldn't make out exactly what was happening inside the house.

Ciara pointed at the car coming down the road.

"Looks like we won't have to call the cops because here they are."

"Do you think someone in the neighborhood called them or do you think Hope did?"

"I don't know, but either way, Willy isn't going to be very happy about it. With any luck, they'll be taking him out of there. We just have to pray that Hope follows through by pressing charges and finally leaves him for good."

They didn't have to wait very long before they got their

answer. Two police officers walked a handcuffed Willy McKenna to their cruiser. He was swearing loudly for everyone to hear. Hope stood in the doorway watching but said nothing. As soon as the police car left, Ciara and Sarah jumped out of the car and walked quickly to Hope's house. She had gone back inside, so they rang the doorbell.

Hope came to the door holding a bag of peas on her left cheek. As soon as she saw Sarah and Ciara, she started to cry and fell into Sarah's arms.

"It's ok, sweetie. Everything is going to be ok."

Ciara waited for Hope to stop crying before she started asking questions.

"Hope, how did the police know Willy was hitting you? Did you call them?"

She nodded. "I called 911 from my cell phone and left it sitting on the kitchen counter so they could hear everything."

Sarah smiled. "That was very brave of you."

The three women sat in silence for a while, letting Hope regain her strength.

"If you and Ms. Moretti can wait for me, I'd like to pack my bags and go back to the shelter with you. Would that be all right?"

Sarah hugged Hope and nodded. "You bet."

While Hope got her things, Sarah looked at Ciara and smiled. "We did a good thing today."

Ciara shook her head. "No, honey. You did a good thing; I just rode shotgun."

CHAPTER 11

*B*eth opened the front door so that her boyfriend, Gabriel could carry the Christmas tree into the living room. The balsam fir smell immediately filled the room and brought back memories of her childhood. She didn't have to think about where to place the tree because, growing up, the family tree always sat in front of the window facing the street. Now that she and her brother Christopher lived in the house, their family traditions could continue.

Christopher came out of the kitchen and watched his sister and her boyfriend adjust the tree upright. He leaned against the wall and held his hands up, his fingers formed to produce a frame.

"Stand back everyone and let the expert handle this. It needs to go a little to the left."

After giving his opinion, Christopher sat on the sofa and opened a magazine.

Her hands on her hips, Beth teased her brother.

"Just because you've got only one leg doesn't mean you get to sit on your behind and bark out instructions. If you can run a marathon, you can help with a Christmas tree. Get up."

Christopher laughed at Beth. "I knew you couldn't do it without me."

A cold wind blowing through the house, Christopher's girlfriend, Becca came through the front door.

"Whoa. It's freezing out there. I know you all are used to winters in Massachusetts but for this Florida girl, it's awful. I'm chilled to the bone. Maybe we should light a fire."

Gabriel came out from behind the tree.

"I second that."

Christopher got up from the sofa and kissed Becca.

"How about we get more wood from the pile outside and I'll get the fire going?"

"Sounds good. After that, I think hot chocolate is in order."

Beth's cell phone buzzed. It was their brother Michael, who sounded like he was out of breath.

"Hey big brother. What's going on over at your house? You sound like you've been running."

"Quinn and Cora are chasing me around the sofa. I think it's time to get back to the gym. When you can't keep up with eight- and six-year-olds, you know you're in trouble. What are you guys doing at your house?"

"Gabriel and I just got our Christmas tree up and Chris and Becca are getting wood for a fire. The only thing left is Christmas music which I'm about to play any minute. You know how much us Wheelers love Christmas music."

"Sounds like fun. That's exactly why I'm calling."

"Huh?"

"You better put me on speaker phone so Chris can hear too."

She put her phone on speaker and called Chris to come back inside.

Chris came into the house with a pile of wood in his arms, followed by Becca who carried several logs.

"Michael is on speaker."

"Hey Michael, what's up?"

"Mom's calling a Code Red."

"What? Is she all right?"

"Yeah, it's not for her, it's for Lauren, Olivia, and Lily. Lauren left Jeff and flew down to Florida and didn't tell anyone."

Beth dropped to the sofa and put her hand to her forehead. Chris and Becca sat next to her. Gabriel sat in the corner chair and motioned to his dog, Charlie to sit quietly on his dog bed.

"You're kidding me."

"I wish I were. Looks like Jeff is having an affair."

Beth couldn't believe what she was hearing. She'd always admired Lauren and Jeff's marriage and hoped she'd be as lucky as her big sister when it came to a stable relationship.

"This is bad, Michael. Chris and I have been over there, and they've come here for dinners and just to hang out, but we haven't been there for several weeks because the tension was so bad. I knew there was trouble, but I had no idea that Jeff was cheating on her."

Chris agreed. "It's been really rough watching the two of them go at each other. Now that you're telling us this, I'm starting to piece together several comments. I just can't believe Jeff would do this to Lauren, not to mention Olivia and Lily."

"Mom wants us all down in Captiva for Christmas to be there for Lauren, and I think it's a good idea. Trust me, Brea and I wanted to stay home this year and have Christmas be a quiet one, but our sister is going to need all the support she can get."

Beth looked at Gabriel for his reaction. They had planned to celebrate Christmas with his brother's family. Now, this latest drama put that at risk.

Gabriel smiled and nodded his head. "It's ok, Beth. Your sister needs you. It's fine."

Beth was on board, but when she looked at Christopher, he was quick to give his opinion.

"Michael, what do you think about the two of us going over to Jeff's place to confront him?"

"Honestly, Chris that was my first reaction too, but Mom said she thought that would be a mistake because Lauren hasn't talked to him yet."

The room went silent for a minute before Beth spoke.

"What do you mean she hasn't talked to him? Didn't she confront him?"

"Apparently not."

"Oh, for heaven's sake. What could she be thinking? I feel like calling her myself."

Michael cautioned against that.

"Nothing by phone is going to work. Don't forget that Mom called a Code Red. You know what that means."

"What's a Code Red?" Becca asked.

Chris answered her. "It basically means all hands-on deck. All our lives when one of us was in trouble or needed the support of the whole family, we'd call a Code Red. There's no other solution when that happens. If we don't go down to Florida to support Lauren and my nieces, that's tantamount to being excommunicated from the family."

Becca's face looked like she'd just eaten something disgusting, and so, Beth tried to lessen the severity of Christopher's statement.

"Really, Chris? I wouldn't go that far."

She looked at Becca and tried to explain.

"We're a close family, Becca. This is just Mom's way of getting us all to come down to Captiva."

"Beth!" Michael yelled through the phone.

"What?"

"You're being unfair. Lauren's going through a really bad time. I think you're being a bit insensitive about this."

"Listen, guys. I feel bad for what Lauren and Jeff are going through, but hasn't it occurred to any of you that Mom is calling a Code Red so that we'll all be with her at Christmas? I'm just being practical. You can't tell me that it hasn't crossed your mind."

No one wanted to admit that Beth might be right, so when no one responded, she gave up.

"I'll do whatever the majority rules, but I'm still a little skeptical."

Christopher looked at Becca and then at Beth. His face looked sad.

"If you're right, then I think it's even more important that the whole family is together this year. Maybe Mom needs us more than Lauren does."

Christopher's words made Beth feel awful for not recognizing their mother's cry for help.

"I didn't think of it that way. What do you think, Michael?"

"I think Chris is right. No matter what, this family needs to be together and that means both Gabriel and Becca should be there too. You guys are family now, whether you want to be or not. Are you guys in?"

Becca and Gabriel looked at each other and smiled. In unison, they agreed to join the Wheeler clan for Christmas. Gabriel had food on his mind.

"I'm happy to support your family in any way that I can. Besides, I can't wait to see what delicious holiday meals Riley and Grace will create."

Beth shook her head.

"I can't believe you just said that."

"I'm looking forward to seeing my family as well. I have to imagine that my father and brothers have lost lots of weight since I've been living in Massachusetts. If nothing else, my coming home will probably save them before they waste away." Becca said.

Michael laughed.

"Then it's settled. I'll give Mom a call and let her know. Our next problem is finding flights that still have seats available. I'm not sure we'll all be able to get on the same plane, but if we can, that would be preferable. We're going to need to find either a house to rent or hotel rooms nearby. Before Lauren and the girls showed up, all the rooms at the inn were booked until Christmas. Lauren's staying at Chelsea's for now."

Beth had an idea.

"Why don't you guys let me try to book the flight. I've got connections through work that might help, and Becca and I will see what we can find on VRBO and Airbnb."

"That sounds great. Get back to me as soon as you can, and thanks guys. I think we're doing the right thing. Operation Code Red is on."

Beth rolled her eyes and looked at her Christmas tree. They'd need to decorate it right away so that she could take a picture with her phone. If she wasn't going to enjoy it in person, the least she could do was to look at it while celebrating Christmas on Captiva Island.

CHAPTER 12

he first time Maggie felt the lump was in the shower. Thinking it was nothing, she continued to do as she always did, focus on others instead of herself. The second time she had to acknowledge that something was wrong. She didn't want to make a fuss or worry Paolo, so she made an appointment with her doctor without telling him.

After the mammogram and subsequent biopsy, she thought it best to tell Paolo given the bandage on her breast and her anxious demeanor.

"I'm sure it's nothing."

Paolo nodded in agreement, but she could see that he was concerned. Maggie didn't want to ruin the family Christmas celebrations and so she decided that if it was cancer, she'd wait until after everyone returned home. She'd deal with doctor's appointments and treatment in the new year if need be.

When the result of the biopsy came back as cancer, Maggie and Paolo together made the decision for her to have a lumpectomy. At first, Paolo was uncomfortable giving his advice. He felt it was her body and as such she should be the one to choose, but Maggie wouldn't hear of it. She'd come to rely on him for his wisdom and strength, and never before did she need those two things as much as she did now.

Unfortunately, radiation would first be needed to shrink the tumor so that the surgeon could remove the cancer completely. Scheduling those appointments would be tricky with family visiting. In the end they booked Maggie's first treatment during the week between Christmas and New Year.

With Lauren's troubles and the calling of Code Red, Maggie decided that she would tell her children about the cancer, but not until the very last minute. There was so much to do with decorations and wrapping of presents, not to mention she still had guests to attend to. The holiday would be challenging to say the least, but she found comfort in knowing that she'd be surrounded by her family during the most important fight of her life.

A knock on the back door startled Maggie. She was surprised to see Santa Claus standing in her kitchen.

"Hey, Maggie. What do you think?"

Byron was under the Santa suit and was carrying bells in his hand. He shook them as he bellowed, "Ho, Ho, Ho."

Since there never was a meal or piece of pie that he would ever refuse, Byron filled the suit perfectly.

"Byron, I think you were born to be Santa Claus. You look amazing."

He twirled around so that she could get a good look at the entire outfit.

"Marcus Werner wanted to be Santa this year, but I got to it first. I think he's a little put out about the whole thing, but I don't care."

"Maybe you and Marcus can trade off years. You be Santa this year and he can do it next year."

"Maggie, my dear. Have you ever seen Marcus as Santa? He's done it before but everyone on the island knows he's not very good at it. First of all, he's way too skinny, and second, he's more of a grinch than a Santa. He doesn't have the jolly part down the way I do. You can't walk around the island being grumpy and still yell out Ho, Ho, Ho."

Maggie had to agree with Byron. Marcus Werner was a miserable old man. That he had any interest at all in playing Santa surprised her.

"Well, maybe to keep him happy, you could ask him to be an elf or something. Give him another important position during the Christmas Festival or he'll be complaining the whole day."

Byron pulled his Santa beard down under his chin.

"Speaking of the Festival, and I don't want to be a pest, but you are the only inn owner on the island who hasn't responded to my request to represent your business in the parade. It's only five days away you know. All the other Bed and Breakfasts have agreed to participate. What about the Key Lime Garden Inn?"

Maggie didn't really want to participate in the parade. She felt the inn was an elegant property with discriminating guests. Walking in the parade felt like she was standing on the sidewalk trying to get people to come inside. It was beneath her, and beneath the inn's reputation.

"Oh, Byron. We will be so busy with our guests. I'm totally booked. I'm not sure I can find the time. We'd have to get costumes or at the very least some sort of banner. Besides, I can't afford to let anyone take the time off to walk in the parade. I need all my workers leading right up to Christmas, and then my family arrives. It's just too much."

She could see his disappointment but didn't know what else to say.

"Would you like some coffee and Christmas cookies? Riley just pulled them out of the oven."

His head down, he walked to the stove and took a reindeer-shaped cookie from the tray.

"Do you think I could have a glass of milk?"

"Of course. You sit at the table and let me get that for you."

Maggie felt awful that she'd broken Santa's spirit, but the

truth was that with her new diagnosis it was going to be a difficult holiday for her no matter how hard she tried to push the cancer to the back of her mind. Walking in a parade was the last thing she wanted to do.

The next morning, Sarah bounced up the stairs of the carriage house, calling for Maggie to see what she had made. When she got to the top of the stairs, she twirled around.

"What on earth?"

"I'm an elf. What do you think of my costume? I know it's probably hard to believe, but I made it myself."

"You look adorable."

"Well, guess what? I made one for you too. You can be an elf with me."

"Sarah, why on earth would I want to be an elf?"

"I thought we'd look cute in the parade."

Maggie couldn't believe the subject of the island's Christmas parade was still front and center.

"Why are you walking in the parade exactly?"

"A couple of weeks ago, Byron got in touch with me to ask if I'd like to advertise the Outreach Center during the Christmas Festival. He thought it would be great if we carried a banner in the parade. He said that you'd be doing the same for the inn. I just thought it would be cute if we had something festive to wear."

Maggie was furious.

"Sarah, I never told Byron that. As a matter of fact, we had a talk just yesterday and I told him to forget about including the inn. There's just too much going on. I can't add participating in the Christmas parade along with everything else."

"What do you mean, everything else? Aren't you going to go to the festival at all? Trevor is going to bring Noah and Sophia and watch the parade and I thought I'd go over to Chelsea's and invite Olivia and Lily too. You know how much those girls need some Christmas fun."

Maggie nodded.

"I do indeed. The girls have been asking if they're going to see their father when Christmas comes. They are completely in the dark about what's going on, so of course they just assume Jeff will come to Captiva eventually. It breaks my heart."

With her grandchildren in mind, Maggie saw the parade in a different light. Maybe it was a good idea to join the others participating in the festival. It would be one more thing to distract her from the health concerns.

"Byron told me that he's playing Santa this year and that Santa will be arriving by boat. The whole thing is staged to have the boat come ashore with him at the helm. The boat's going to be filled with gifts. Parents have been shopping for weeks. They've collected all the presents at the town hall. I actually think he's going to need a second boat to help because there are so many boxes. Becca's family, the Powells are donating their time. I think her brother Finn is driving Santa's boat."

Maggie reached for the elf costume.

"Give me that thing. I'll try it on and see how it fits. How did you know my size?"

"Paolo helped me. He gave me one of your dresses."

"I'll have a talk with him later."

Maggie went into her bedroom while Sarah waited for her mother to walk through the living room modeling the costume. She put the outfit on like a coat pushing her arms through the sleeves first. There were clips, buttons, and Velcro and since she couldn't depend on the fabric covering her body it would have to be worn over her regular clothes.

Sarah had done a good job sewing the costume, but when Maggie looked in the full-length mirror she thought she looked stupid.

I'm a woman with breast cancer wearing an elf costume.

It was hard not to laugh at the ridiculousness of her situation. Shaking her head, she unsnapped the costume and pulled it down. Stepping out from the garment she folded it and walked out to the living room.

She handed the ensemble back to Sarah and hugged her.

"Honey, you did a great job on the sewing, but I'm afraid this isn't for me. I promise I'll wear something red and green and look as festive as I can, but I just don't think I was born to be an elf. Why don't you see if Lauren will wear it? I think Olivia and Lily would love seeing their mother as one of Santa's little helpers."

"That's all right Mom. I had a feeling you wouldn't want to wear it. I think it's a great idea for Lauren though. I'm going to run over to Chelsea's and see if I can talk her into it. With Olivia and Lily there I'm sure we can gang up on her. I'll talk to you later."

Maggie watched Sarah walk down the stairs and to her car. She laughed out loud watching her daughter, the pregnant elf, drive down the driveway. She took a deep breath and looked at her watch. There was only one place Byron Jameson would be at this hour, and that was The Bubble Room bar. If she hurried, he might still be sober.

CHAPTER 13

*M*aggie stared at the letter from the doctor. *Ductal carcinoma in situ.* A non-invasive and not aggressive breast cancer. It meant that Maggie was at risk of it becoming invasive breast cancer down the road. The choice was Maggie's, but she could tell that her doctor encouraged a mastectomy rather than a lumpectomy due to the large area of the DCIS. It was, in the doctor's opinion, the reason Maggie felt a lump. Usually, this type of cancer is found during mammography.

Once again she found herself unable to sleep. Rather than sit on the porch swing, she walked down the seashell-lined path to the ocean. As large a problem as the cancer was, when she sat in front of the magnitude of the water, she felt small and insignificant. Her problems became tiny in those moments and that's exactly what she needed in the early morning hours of this new day.

She didn't sit in her usual spot, but instead moved closer to the water, the waves whipping up the surf hitting her face. She tasted the salty wetness and when she could, opened her eyes to watch the storm-infused grayness of the sky. This was her ocean.

She claimed it months ago when she first moved to Captiva. She allowed the tourists to sample its beauty, but it was hers for as long as she walked the earth.

Until now, she hadn't thought much about her own death. Daniel's heart attack forced decisions upon her that she had little control over. She didn't see it coming and wouldn't have known what to do if she had. Now, she needed a plan to save her life, and the process overwhelmed her.

To take my breast or not to take my breast. That was the question, and she didn't know what to do. She could Google information, or she could let the doctor take control. Having someone else drive the bus seemed easier. With so much going on in her life, this would be one decision she could delegate. He was the expert after all.

A smaller voice reminded her of the years of giving up her power and how well that turned out. No, she would have to choose, and a second opinion would help her do that. She'd research doctors to get a second opinion but she felt they'd only confirm what she already knew, that to protect her life, a total mastectomy was the best decision.

Maggie sat on the beach for two hours before the wind picked up, forcing her to run back to the inn just in time to remove the cushions from the outdoor furniture. Paolo ran to help her, and they made it back inside the inn as the darkened sky opened.

He grabbed a towel from the linen closet and ran it over his hair. "The weather forecast isn't looking good for the rest of the day. Good thing the festival wasn't today, or we'd have to cancel."

Two couples were in the library playing cards. Maggie found Riley and Grace preparing lunch.

"What do the two of you think of putting together tea and cookies for the guests after lunch? No one is going out in this weather today. We might as well continue to feed them."

Riley agreed. "No problem at all. Grace and I can do that.

We'll pretend we're in England and are having our afternoon tea. You never know, it just might catch on."

Maggie gave her a thumbs up and then joined Paolo on the porch. They watched heavy streams of water pour down from the awning.

"I think we better wait here until it lightens up don't you?"

Paolo shook his head.

"We'll be stuck here for hours if we do that. How about this? I'll race you to the carriage house. First one there gets a massage from the loser."

"I like it. I plan on getting in the bathtub right after my massage."

She didn't wait for him to say "go", instead she got a jump start and beat him to the carriage house. He'd say her move was unfair, but she didn't care. She'd get that massage one way or the other before the day was over.

Not wanting to disturb Chelsea, Lauren quietly walked out onto the lanai and watched the rain fall. Olivia and Lily were coloring at the kitchen table and Chelsea was deep in thought as she worked on her painting. Lauren's cell phone buzzed, and the sound made Chelsea turn around.

Seeing Callum Foster's name, Lauren didn't answer the call.

"I'm sorry, Chelsea, I didn't mean to interrupt your work."

"You're not interrupting me. Who was that on the phone? Was it Jeff?"

Lauren felt embarrassed, and all she could do was say, "No."

Now it was Chelsea's turn to feel embarrassed.

"I'm sorry, Lauren. That was none of my business."

Lauren hesitated before saying another word.

"I'm not...I don't know how..."

Lauren didn't have a clue how to approach the subject. By

now, Callum Foster had to know that she'd left Massachusetts. Lauren explained to Nell that although Nell could reach her while she was away, she didn't want clients, and especially Callum, to call her cell phone. She regretted letting him into her life, even if it was under the auspice of being her client. They both knew the truth, but Lauren refused to admit it, even to herself.

Leaving so much unsaid, Lauren unintentionally created a situation that she hadn't anticipated. If Chelsea assumed she'd been unfaithful to her husband, Lauren needed to clear that up. She sat next to Chelsea trying to find the right words, but soon realized that what she was about to say was not for Chelsea's benefit, but her own. Had she been unfaithful? She thought about her time with Callum and wondered if she'd done anything to lead him on?

Chelsea put her paintbrush down and turned to face her.

"I'm guessing that wasn't your husband on the phone."

Lauren shook her head.

"No, it wasn't"

"Why don't you start from the beginning, Lauren? I'm not here to pass judgment, but if you need someone to talk to who isn't your mother, I'm available."

Lauren laughed.

"Mom isn't as bad as I make her out to be. It's just that when I was here for Sarah's wedding, I sort of mentioned a guy at my office who was hitting on me. I fired him, actually."

"You fired someone because he was hitting on you?"

"No. I fired him because he was bad at his job. The hitting on me part was just annoying most of the time."

"Most? Not all?"

"I guess I'm guilty of liking the attention. I mentioned it to my mother, and she figured where there's smoke…"

"Well, Maggie was right. Having someone around who makes you feel all warm and fuzzy while you're having troubles at home isn't always a smart thing. Was that who was on the phone?"

Lauren got up from her chair. "No."

"Someone else?"

Lauren explained about Callum Foster and when she finished, she waited for Chelsea's reaction.

"This Callum seems to be more invested in you than you in him. Shouldn't you tell him so?"

"Of course. It's just…"

"It feels good to be pursued when you're attracted to the pursuer. Don't you agree?"

"Honestly, Chelsea, I love Jeff, and I haven't stopped even after finding him with someone else. I have zero interest in Callum except for the fact that I used him to get back at Jeff. Even though we didn't do anything, I felt vengeful and righteous about it too. But you're right. I've got to tell Callum what I'm feeling. I love Jeff but I'm so angry at him. How could he do this to me?"

"Lauren, at the risk of playing devil's advocate, you don't know a thing about what Jeff has done. You saw him in a restaurant with a woman you've never seen before. Isn't it possible that it was completely innocent?"

"You should have seen them together, Chelsea. It didn't look innocent to me."

"Then tell me this. Can you be sure that Jeff didn't do anything more than what you did with Callum? Maybe he was feeling special because this woman is interested in him. It doesn't mean he wants to be with her. What if Jeff saw you with Callum? Can you imagine what he might think? Callum is calling your cell phone. I'd say that's at least one step more than that woman did."

"Oh, Come on, Chelsea. Callum is a client."

"Really? According to you he was a complete stranger you met at the mall. What do you really know about him? Isn't it possible that you are as much to blame for this mix-up between you and your husband as Jeff is?"

Chelsea was right. Lauren knew only what Callum had told her about his life. Whatever his motivation, she couldn't be certain that he was her client because he wanted to get to know her more than his desire to find a place to live.

And here she was on Captiva Island getting phone calls from this man. She knew perfectly well that the appearance of impropriety was almost as bad as the real thing. She was wholly complicit in the flirtation that had gone on between her and Callum. At the very least, Jeff had the right to defend himself, and she had no right to feel justified in her actions.

"I should call Jeff."

Chelsea tapped Lauren's knee. "Sounds like the right move to me."

Lauren loved the way Chelsea didn't let her emotions get in the way of her advice. If she had talked to her mother, the outcome might have been completely different.

"Thank you, Chelsea."

"Don't thank me. Thank those two little girls in the living room. They should be the reasons for everything you do."

Lauren smiled and hugged Chelsea. How lucky her mother was to have such a devoted and loving friend nearby she was just beginning to understand.

CHAPTER 14

*B*eth closed the door of her car with her foot and walked toward her front door carrying bags filled with Christmas presents. Her toes cold inside her boots, she looked forward to warming them and the rest of her body in a hot tub filled with lavender-scented water.

A tall woman with long blonde wavy hair stood in front of the house waiting for someone to answer the door.

Beth called out to her. "Hello? Can I help you?"

The woman turned and smiled. "Hey, Beth. I just rang the doorbell thinking I might catch you at home. How are you?"

Emily Wheeler, Beth's half-sister looked beautiful bundled in her faux-fur coat and boots. She was the spitting image of Beth, and everyone thought they were twins.

"Emily! Wow, this is a surprise. Why didn't you let me know you were coming? I would have stayed home and prepared something for us. All I can manage after all this shopping is maybe a couple of pizzas"

"Don't worry about me. I just wanted to stop in and run something by you if you've got a few minutes."

"Of course, let's get inside and out of this cold. You must be freezing. How long have you been standing there? Christopher must not be home."

"Christopher is here?"

Beth dropped the bags as soon as they entered the house. Taking her coat and hat off, she grabbed Emily's and hung them in the closet.

"Yes, I'm sorry I didn't update you on this. I guess I dropped the ball on staying in touch with you. I'm sorry about that. Chris moved back home after his time recuperating in Florida. He's doing really well. I'm so excited that you're here because you'll finally get to meet him."

"I can't wait. I hope he'll show up before I leave."

"Can I get you anything? I was thinking of making a cup of hot chocolate. Any chance I can convince you to join me?"

"Thanks. I'd love a cup."

As she prepared the hot chocolate, Beth thought about her first encounter with Emily last year. The entire family was shocked to hear that their father had an affair that produced a daughter. It took some time but at Emily's initial request to get to know her siblings, everyone in the family made a great effort to accept her. Beth felt bad that she had let so many months pass without communicating with the young woman.

When the hot chocolate was ready, Beth filled two large mugs to the top.

"Do you want marshmallows?"

"No, thanks. Just plain."

Beth carried the cups into the living room and handing Emily her mug, sat next to her on the sofa.

"So, what brings you to Andover?"

"I guess you could say, Christmas. Mom has been seeing this new guy and wants to spend the holiday with him skiing in Park City, Utah. She's practically forcing me to go with her."

"Would that really be such a bad thing? I've heard Park City is beautiful. Lots of great restaurants and shopping. It's not all skiing."

Emily rolled her eyes.

"No. It would be terrible. First of all, I'm not crazy about him…Arthur. He's got a terrible laugh and always talks with his mouth full. It's disgusting."

Beth laughed at her sister's animated expressions.

"Maybe you could go off by yourself and meet people. I bet they just want your approval of the relationship."

"I honestly don't care at all who my mother dates. If Arthur is her cup of tea then so be it. I'm perfectly happy to give her my approval if she needs it, but I don't want to spend the holiday with him. I shouldn't be forced to after all. I'm an adult and might have plans of my own."

"Do you have somewhere you'd rather go for Christmas?"

Emily took a sip of her hot chocolate and then, with a sweet and innocent face, looked up from her cup and dropped the bomb.

"I want to spend Christmas with you and the rest of our brothers and sisters."

Beth immediately felt awful. Her little sister wanted to be with her siblings this Christmas, and she was about to turn her away.

"Oh, Emily. I'm so sorry, but I don't think that can happen."

"You mean because of your mother, Maggie? I know we haven't met yet, but I know she'll love me once she gets to know me. I do understand how difficult it must be to accept a child from an affair, but I think we can all agree that it isn't my fault how I came into the world."

Beth understood why Emily would take her response as a reflection of their feelings for her. She quickly needed to put Emily's fears at rest.

"No. It's nothing like that. I'm sure Mom will love you just as much as the rest of us do. The problem is that none of us will be home for Christmas. We're all going down to Captiva to be with Mom and her new husband, Paolo. It's been a few years since we've all been together for the holiday."

The front door blew open and Christopher and Becca came inside the house along with a bit of snow.

Becca took her hat and mittens off.

"I can't believe this weather. The snow is falling again. They say it will only be a few inches but by the looks of what's out there and with this wind it seems like the beginning of something bigger."

Beth couldn't wait to introduce Christopher and his girlfriend to Emily.

"Chris, this is our sister, Emily."

Emily got up from the sofa and ran over to her brother. Right from the start she'd never been shy meeting any of her siblings, and this time was no different. They hugged and Christopher stood back to look at her.

"I swear you're the spitting image of Beth. You two could be twins."

"I know. Isn't that cool? I knew the first time I met her that we were related. This is Becca? Nice to meet you."

"It's very nice to meet you, too, Emily. You live in Hingham, right?"

"Yes, with my mother."

"That's a bit of a drive isn't it? With this weather you might find yourself stuck in Andover for the night. I'm not sure I'd drive back down to Hingham in this."

Beth joined them. "That's a great idea. Why don't you stay the night? It will give you and Chris a chance to get to know each other, and I'd love to catch up with you."

Emily nodded. "I'd love to. I'll give my mom a call and let her know so she won't worry."

"Let's go upstairs and I'll show you your room. You probably don't have any clothes, so I'll get you something to wear to sleep in."

Emily laughed at the suggestion. "Confession time, you don't have to do that. I've got my bag in the car. I packed my toothbrush and everything. I was hoping you'd ask me to stay."

Beth laughed and shook her head. Her sister was more like her than she realized.

Beth gave Emily privacy to talk with her mother. In the meantime, she took the opportunity to go downstairs and talk to Christopher about Emily's Christmas wish.

"I feel bad that she can't be with us, but it's out of our control."

Christopher wasn't so convinced.

"Why can't she be with us? Mom called a Code Red, right? That means the whole family needs to be together. Emily is our sister, so why not include her?"

"Chris, do I really have to explain to you why this is a bad idea? Mom hasn't even met Emily yet, and to be honest we can't just show up with our mother's dead-cheating-almost-ex-husband's-illegitimate child."

Emily gave a thumbs up as she walked down the stairs.

"All set. Let me get my stuff out of the car. Be right back."

Christopher whispered,

"Calm down. I'm not suggesting we just show up with her. I think if we call Mom and explain the situation, she'll have the opportunity to say yes or no. We don't say anything to Emily until we know for sure. Besides, how do you even know if her mother will agree? Didn't you say she wants to take Emily to Park City?"

Beth nodded. "She does, but Emily is an adult. She's over eighteen and can make her own decision. I just hope that her mother understands that we're not trying to pull Emily away from her. I'll have to explain to Emily that she better tell her mother this was her idea and not ours. Why don't you and Becca entertain her while I go in my bedroom and call Mom? We need to deal with this right away."

Beth grabbed her cell phone and headed upstairs to her bedroom.

When Beth explained to Maggie what they were planning, a long pause on the other end of the line had her worried.

"Mom, you don't have to do this. I know you've probably got a lot of stress dealing with Lauren at the same time as taking care of your guests. You can say no, and no one will be the wiser. Chris and I thought we should ask you and let you decide."

Her mother finally spoke. "I feel bad for Emily. She never really got a chance to be close with her father, and now her mother is off with a new man. You and your brothers and sisters have done a lovely thing by giving Emily a real family. You are right, she is part of our family and as such should be treated that way."

"So, you're saying we should bring her with us?"

"I am."

"Are you sure?"

"Beth, I've taught you kids to be generous with your possessions and your time. My children are caring, loving and compassionate people and I'm proud of you all. I've watched you welcome complete strangers into our home when they were down on their luck or just didn't have any family. I laugh when I think of all the strays that have entered the Wheeler home. Some were furry, and others not so much. How can I do any different?"

"I'm the one who's proud, Mom. I think you're wonderful and deserve only the best."

"Thank you, honey. We'll see if your grandmother agrees with you. I'm about to call her to invite her down. I know she can be a handful, but it wouldn't be the whole family without her. I'll be counting on you all to get her down here. I'll call you tomorrow after I've talked to her. Wish me luck."

"Sounds great. Good luck, Mom."

Beth laughed when she ended the call. She could hear her grandmother's voice. *"I wondered when you'd get around to calling your mother. It's Christmas for heaven's sake. What took you so long?"*

She joined the others in the living room and gave Christopher a look that said, "you win."

She then looked at Emily and smiled.

"Emily, how would you like to spend this Christmas on Captiva Island, Florida?"

Placing her hands on her head, Emily looked ecstatic. "Are you serious? You want me to go with you to Florida?"

Beth nodded. "If your mother agrees. I've just called my mom and she said to come along."

Christopher and Becca laughed watching Emily's excitement.

"I can't believe this. Yes, of course. I'd love to go. This is incredible. I'll have to get my summer clothes down from the attic. When do we leave?"

Beth gave Emily all the travel details that she received from Michael. Everyone had been able to get seats on two flights arriving on December 21st. Except for the grandchildren, most were single seats, but they took them anyway. Now, with Emily and their grandmother added to the group, Beth would have to talk to Michael to find two more seats. The way Emily was acting, she wasn't going to miss this opportunity even if it meant sitting amongst the luggage in the belly of the plane.

Christmas this year was shaping up to look like none that had gone before, but whether that was a good thing or not was anyone's guess.

CHAPTER 15

*L*auren's days on Captiva were filled with quiet introspection and hours dedicated to being with her children. Most days she got out of bed at seven o'clock, and like her mother, Lauren found comfort in the solitude of early morning walks on the beach. She had much to think about, not the least of which was her failing marriage and inability to confront her husband.

Her talk with Chelsea helped her gain perspective on her situation, and she was committed to reaching out with a call to Jeff after her walk. Lauren wasn't sure sharing her feelings with him on the phone was a good idea, but it was all she could do thanks to her fleeing Massachusetts so quickly.

The cell phone in her pocket vibrated with a call from Sarah.

"Hey, I see I'm not the only one up this early."

"I've got a busy day, so I thought I'd talk to you before I head to the office. What are you doing today?"

"Oh, I'm guessing the same thing I've been doing every day since I got here. Doing an imitation of the walking wounded, which isn't easy to do with all the Christmas cheer surrounding the island."

ANNIE CABOT

"That's what I thought. How about I come and get you and you can hang with me instead?"

"Aren't you working today?"

"I am, but it dawned on me that you've never seen where I work or what I do. I thought it might be a nice distraction and I could use the help quite frankly. Can Chelsea watch Olivia and Lily for a few hours?"

Since she'd come to the island, Lauren had stayed close to the inn. Going off-island to spend the day with Sarah when she didn't feel like interacting with anyone wasn't appealing.

"I don't know, Sarah. I'm not very good company these days."

"Great, then you'll be in good company."

"Huh?"

"Trust me, Lauren. Take a few hours to get away from your thoughts and let me take control. It won't hurt, I promise."

Lauren laughed at that. She was used to being the big sister and the one with all the answers. As confused as Lauren was, letting her baby sister take care of her for a while felt comforting.

"All right. Let me talk to Chelsea and I'll text you."

"Sounds good. See if Paolo or mom can drive you to the bridge. I can pick you up there. It would save me a bunch of driving. I won't leave my house until I hear from you."

"Will do."

When Lauren asked Chelsea if she could watch the girls, she didn't expect her response.

"Did you call Jeff?"

"No. Not yet. I was going to call him this morning, but now that I'm spending the day with Sarah, I thought I'd wait."

It wasn't an admonishment but more like a warning when Chelsea said, "I wouldn't wait too long."

What did she mean by that, exactly?

Rather than get into a deep conversation with Chelsea, Lauren decided to ignore the comment and focus on the day.

Whatever Sarah had in store for her, she'd go with the flow and pray for clarity and confidence when she finally did call Jeff.

The sign outside the building didn't give away the property's true function. *A Way Home* could have been an orphanage or a restaurant. For most who found their way inside, the safe haven was an oasis—a place to not only call home but a protection from the violence they had endured.

Sarah led Lauren inside and they entered a room with several women and children who were playing. A wall lined with raincoats, umbrellas and personal items reflected the enormity of the community need. The shelter was full with very few openings left.

Sarah motioned for Lauren to join her in the small kitchen.

"We're fully booked is one way to put it. But this is nothing like a hotel."

"Are they all women and children? Are there any men here?"

"Only women at this shelter. While it's true that anyone can be a victim of domestic violence, there seems to be a higher rate of incidence among women and girls."

Hope McKenna emptied the coffeepot and washed it.

"Hello, Ms. Hutchins. I'm going to make another pot of coffee if you can wait a bit for it to brew."

"Hi, Hope. Yes, thanks. This is my sister, Lauren. She's visiting from Massachusetts."

Hope stopped what she was doing and turned to Lauren. "Nice to meet you."

"It's lovely to meet you, Hope. Are you here alone or do you have children with you?"

Hope shook her head. "No, I don't have children."

Her face looked sad. "I was pregnant once, but I miscarried."

Lauren felt awful for asking. "Oh, I'm so sorry."

She looked at Sarah and then back again at Lauren. "It's ok. You didn't know. I didn't know Ms. Hutchins back then. I guess if I did, my baby would have lived. My husband kicked me in my stomach. I think he hated both me and the baby. I don't know. I finally found this place. Your sister saved my life. I'll be forever grateful to her."

A lump formed in Lauren's throat. She didn't know what to say, but she was proud of Sarah and wondered how many women she'd saved in the short time she'd lived in Florida.

Lauren walked to Sarah and put her arm around her sister.

"Yes, she's a good person. I'm very proud of her, and I'm glad she was able to help you. I had a miscarriage too. Of course, it wasn't the same thing as what you went through, but it was a terrible loss. The one thing that helped me was to think that one day, I'll see my baby again. I truly believe that."

Losing her child was something Lauren shared only with their mother. She could tell by the look on Sarah's face that she should have told her before sharing it with Hope, but it felt right to tell her. She wanted to give Hope something to hold onto, and a belief that she'll see her child once again was all she could think to share.

Hope nodded. "I think I believe that too. Would you like to help us decorate the Christmas tree? We're playing Christmas carols and singing too. The ceilings are really high in this building, so we got a pretty tall tree. We need all the help we can get, especially from tall people."

The three women laughed at that. Sarah encouraged Lauren to join in.

"I'd love to."

"Great. Let me finish getting this coffee ready, and I'll take you inside. Ms. Hutchins, are you going to join us?"

"I sure will. Lauren and I would love a cup of coffee before we join you. I'm going to show Lauren around first."

The coffee brewed and Hope left Lauren and Sarah to continue with the tour.

"I can't believe that someone could be so cruel to such a sweet girl."

Sarah agreed. "Hope has been through a lot, but her situation is not unique. So many abused women have similar stories. It's almost like the men can walk into a room full of women and know exactly which ones they can manipulate or influence. Hope has little family and they're on the other side of the country. Cousins mostly who aren't really in her life. Her husband was able to isolate her from any friends in her life; he started with verbal abuse, telling her she was incompetent and stupid, finding fault almost daily. It wasn't long before the physical abuse took over."

Lauren thought of Jeff and her two girls. She'd never been subjected to such cruelty and couldn't fathom a husband hurting his wife. Her marriage was struggling but they were far removed from anything as drastic as that.

"It sounds like Hope is lucky to be alive. At least she can begin a new life with the shelter's help."

Sarah nodded. "I've stayed awake at night thinking about the women who we couldn't save. It's my motivation to keep working to help those who need it. It's not easy, but it's some of the most important work I'll ever do. This, and being a mother and wife. I feel privileged to be a part of it."

They walked back to the kitchen to get their coffee.

"So, are you ready to decorate the tree and sing Christmas carols?"

Lauren smiled. "I'm ready. Lead on."

Jingle Bells came through the speakers and a large crowd gathered around the Christmas tree. Sarah introduced Lauren to everyone, and she was welcomed with open arms.

A teenage girl at a table pulled a ceramic candy cane out of a box and with a marker wrote Lauren's name on it. A red striped ribbon at the top created a loop to attach onto the tree. She handed the ornament to Lauren.

"Here you go. You can put it anywhere on the tree."

Hundreds of similar ornaments, all with the names of the women and children living at the shelter, adorned the tree. Lauren found an open spot and Sarah did the same with hers. After they added their decoration they stepped back to admire the balsam fir.

Lauren reached for her cell phone.

"I want to take a picture. This is a memory I want to keep."

The children quieted and the ceiling lights were dimmed as the tree's red, gold, green, blue, and purple colors glowed. Silent Night filled the room and young and old joined their voices to sing.

In the early morning of her day, Lauren believed her life was spiraling out of control and there was nothing she could do about it. But all that changed as soon as she looked outside her situation and opened her heart to others less fortunate.

Sarah introduced Lauren to a place and people who would help her to see the love and safety of her world. The Christmas tree that stood before her was a reminder of the purpose of the season. In the generosity of the shelter, she found herself not only willing, but anxious to talk to Jeff as soon as she returned to Chelsea's house.

She put her arms around her sister. Once again, her family had come to the rescue.

"Merry Christmas, Sarah, and thank you."

"Merry Christmas, Lauren."

CHAPTER 16

he Key Lime Garden Inn looked so festive that Maggie wondered if they might have overdone it. With the pressure from Byron and the large number of lights that Paolo and Trevor bought, she made a joke that the island couldn't support her electricity needs.

Chelsea stood in the driveway with Maggie and shrugged.

"Well, no one can say you didn't put in an effort this year."

Maggie rolled her eyes.

"It's that darn Byron. I thought it was just me he was fussing about. It seems that the Sea Castle Inn and Pelican Pass were both admonished for their lack of Christmas spirit. I think he played us all."

"Byron's both a menace and a charmer. Seems unfair you've got to keep the lights on all day long."

"I know, but with the festival we really have no choice. I've got to get inside and put on something red. I was going to go with green, but my stomach hasn't felt that great and green makes my face look sick. Did I tell you that Sarah and Lauren are going to be elves in the parade?"

Chelsea laughed. "Yes, Lauren told me. I think it's adorable.

Olivia and Lily are going to go crazy when they see their mother in her elf costume. Lauren's going to come over here to get changed. She thought it would be fun to surprise the girls. They won't see her until she walks past them in the parade."

"By the way, Chelsea, thanks so much for helping Lauren and the girls. You've been wonderful during this whole thing. I appreciate you watching them during the parade."

"Of course. I've enjoyed having them here. By the way, I think I should tell you that Lauren called Jeff last night. She had every intention of getting to the bottom of things."

"How did it go?"

"It didn't. Jeff wasn't answering his phone. I guess when he didn't answer the call or her text, she tried the house land line. He didn't answer there either."

"Oh, no. Now, what?"

"Well, her first instinct was to assume that he was with 'her' and unable to answer the phone. When I told her not to jump to any conclusion, she said that if Jeff didn't feel guilty, he'd have no problem talking to her. The fact that he wouldn't speak to her she feels is a sign that she was right all along."

"Chelsea, this is terrible. I've wanted to give Jeff a call myself but waited for Lauren to talk to him first. Even Michael and Christopher wanted to go over to his house to confront him, but I told them they should wait. Maybe I was wrong. If he won't talk to Lauren, he's got to talk to someone. Lauren can't go on like this. She needs closure one way or the other."

"I agree. When she came home from being with Sarah yesterday, she was in great spirits. She told me that she was going to talk to Jeff and that they would work things out or not, but at least they all wouldn't be hanging in this awful limbo. She wanted to tell Jeff that she'd made a mistake in leaving the way that she did, but she never got the chance."

"Did she at least leave a message?"

Chelsea shook her head. "Nope. She hung up the phone and

her anger returned. It's a setback for sure."

"I've got to talk to her, but I don't think I should right before the parade, do you?"

"Beats me. Maybe you shouldn't talk to her today. It's bad enough that you're grumpy. I don't think a miserable elf is going to help the situation. Let her at least try to be cheerful for her children."

"I'm not grumpy. You'll see. I'll walk in that parade smiling my face off."

"Oh, the girls and I won't be the only witnesses to your acting. Paolo, Trevor, Noah, and Sophia will be standing with us. Who's carrying the inn's banner?"

"Riley and Grace. I walk in front of them and wave."

Chelsea rummaged through her handbag. "Oh, I almost forgot. You have to wear this."

She handed Maggie a red Santa hat with a fully white snow-ball at the end. "Lauren and Sarah's rules. They said if you won't be an elf, the least you can do is wear a Santa hat."

Maggie put the hat on her head.

"How do I look?"

"Well, it's ok I guess. It wouldn't hurt you to smile."

Maggie smiled as broadly as she could and started for the carriage house.

"I'll see you at the parade."

Chelsea yelled back. "You'll recognize your family. We'll be jingling bells. Trevor is bringing them."

Maggie was determined to keep her sanity today. Regardless of her Grinch-like mood, everyone around her was excited about the festival. With Lauren's failed attempt at healing her marriage she needed to be there for her daughter.

Maggie hoped the crowd's festive mood was contagious and somewhere between the Tween Waters Inn and the South Seas Resort she'd find her Christmas spirit. If not, she'd bring every-body down with her attitude and she couldn't bear that thought.

❋

Sarah and Lauren stopped by the carriage house to change into their elf costumes. Maggie bit her tongue and didn't say a word about what had transpired between Lauren and Jeff the night before. She breathed a sigh of relief when Lauren shared her feelings with her.

"I'm so sorry that happened, Lauren, but I'm glad that you at least reached out to Jeff. We still don't know all the facts, and I'm convinced that when the time is right, the two of you will come to an understanding. Don't give up. If you want to keep your marriage, then my advice is to fight for it."

"I know, Mom. It's just that I worry it won't be enough. What happens when only one person is doing the fighting and the other wants to let it all go?"

Maggie didn't have any answers, and it pained her to see the hurt in Lauren's eyes. All she could do was stay positive for her daughter and pray that Jeff would come around.

As difficult as it all was, it was impossible not to laugh at her two daughters in their elf costumes.

"You two look adorable."

Sarah twirled. "Mom, you keep saying that. I think we look authentic."

"Ok, authentically adorable. How's that?"

"Fine. We better get going. I can't wait to see the kids' faces when they see us walking in the parade. Actually, Mom, you are walking, Lauren and I are supposed to sort of dance around. Like pixies."

Lauren looked confused. "Do you really think you should be bouncing around in your condition?"

"Not really. I'm just going to go up and down on my toes and move my arms a lot. You should flit around though. It will look more authentic."

"I thought Santa's elves sat on benches at a table and worked on the toys. I don't remember elves dancing."

Sarah was losing patience.

"Well, we are dancing elves so get used to it. Come on, let's go."

By the time Maggie, Riley and Grace were in their places for the parade, Louise Chambers, Byron's sister, was already barking orders.

"Don't forget to smile and be jolly. When we get to the end near the water, Santa will ride up onto the sand. We don't want to disappoint Santa, now, do we?"

A collective "no" sounded from the crowd, while Maggie rolled her eyes.

Christmas spirit was one thing but knowing that Byron Jameson is inside that Santa suit doesn't make me feel jolly.

Byron had been unbearable and manipulative these last few weeks and Maggie didn't care one bit if Santa was unhappy with her. She smiled, nonetheless.

With the sound of the trumpets and French horns up front, the parade began. Cheers from the crowd, as well as Christmas costumes that some wore, made Maggie laugh. It was easier to accept her marching in the parade as an opportunity to people-watch as much as people were watching her. Every business was lit up with Christmas lights and the sparkling colors made the center of town look more beautiful than usual.

Her family stayed near the end of the parade route partly because they wanted to be near the large island Christmas tree, but also because the kids wanted to be as close as possible to the water and Santa when he arrived.

When they got near the end of the road, Maggie could see Paolo, Chelsea, Trevor, Ciara, and the children waving and shaking their bells. Maggie waved back and even did a little twirl for the crowd. Everyone applauded and then a cheerful roar followed as Santa made his way onto the beach.

Maggie could see Becca's father and brothers driving the boat and helping Santa unload all his gifts. She joined the rest of her family as they made their way closer to the main event. Noah, Olivia, and Lily's faces lit up at the sight of Santa Claus and Trevor picked Noah up and over his shoulders. Paolo and Chelsea lifted Olivia and Lily to help them get a better look.

Noah pointed in excitement.

"Santa Claus is coming. Daddy, it's Santa Claus."

Sarah grabbed Lauren. "Come on, we're supposed to join the other elves and help Santa distribute the gifts."

Lauren looked at her girls. "I'm going to help Santa. I bet he's got something in there for you two. Have you been good?"

Olivia and Lily nodded, their eyes wide in anticipation.

Maggie watched Lauren and Sarah join the other adults who had been cornered into being parade elves. They took gifts from Santa and walked among the crowd calling out the names of children.

Sarah called out, pretending she couldn't see her son.

"Noah Hutchins!"

Noah raised his hand high in the air.

"That's me!"

"Here you go, Noah. This is from Santa Claus."

"Olivia Phillips!"

Olivia jumped up and down as Lauren handed her Santa's gift.

"Lily Phillips!"

"Me! Me!" Lily called out.

"Sophia Hutchins!"

Trevor took the gift for his little girl and winked at Sarah.

"Thank you, cute elf."

For the next thirty minutes, elves helped Santa Claus distribute all the gifts on the boat. When he was done, he waved and yelled, "Merry Christmas. Ho, Ho, Ho. Merry Christmas."

Crawford Powell helped Santa back onto the boat and Finn Powell backed the boat up and out to sea as Santa waved to the crowd.

A band playing Christmas carols moved people to spontaneously sing along, and everyone walked in and out of the gift shops finding last minute items to put under their trees at home.

Paolo put his arms around Maggie as they strolled slowly back to the inn.

"You did well, Mrs. Moretti. You might not have been an elf, but you certainly looked like you were having a good time."

"I have to admit that it was more fun than I thought it would be."

Tears began to fill her eyes.

"What is it, sweetheart?"

Maggie didn't want to bring down the mood, but a single thought wouldn't leave her be. Every day since her diagnosis she'd struggled with worry over it, and she'd told no one. It was the reason she hadn't been able to enjoy the holiday and had little patience for those who walked around spreading cheer and drinking eggnog.

"I don't want this to be my last Christmas."

They stopped in the middle of the road. People walked around them, and Paolo placed his hand on Maggie's face.

"It won't be. We're going to fight this together. You have many more Christmases in your future Mrs. Moretti. You can bet on it."

If love alone could take the cancer from her body, Maggie believed the illness was no match for her family. She knew what was coming in the months ahead and that she would have to find the strength and courage to confront the struggle head-on. This time next year she'd be on the other side of the illness. The cancer would be gone. Maggie could even imagine herself in an elf costume in celebration of her winning the battle, and no one would be happier about that than her.

CHAPTER 17

*C*helsea couldn't remember a time when she had children in the house while wrapping Christmas gifts. Finding a time when everyone was either busy, out of the house or asleep kept her frantic moving wrapping paper, ribbon, and gift tags from room to room. She eventually found the perfect solution and moved everything from her house to Sebastian's.

"I really appreciate this, Sebastian. I've got a couple of sneaky girls in my house who are dying to find anything related to Christmas gifts."

Sebastian sat at the end of the table, watching Chelsea work her decorative magic.

"Anything that gets me more time with you works for me."

Chelsea loved being with Sebastian, and she was happy to have the company while she wrapped presents.

"Not to mention that you're saving Christmas for two little girls. They still believe in Santa Claus, so imagine how disappointed they'd be if I got caught."

"I'm glad you came over because there was something I wanted to ask you."

Chelsea stopped what she was doing and pulled out a chair to sit.

"What's on your mind?"

"We haven't booked our flights and I wondered if there was a problem. If you are having second thoughts…"

"No, not at all. I'm really looking forward to going. I guess I've been so busy with Lauren and the girls staying with me. Honest. Let's get a calendar and pick the date."

"That's another issue I wanted to run by you. Now that I know you have no reservations, I wonder if you would consider leaving sooner rather than later. I have a few business details I need to address, and I need to be in Paris on the 28th."

"Of December?"

"Yes. I know you want to spend Christmas with Maggie and her family, so leaving on that day won't interfere with that. I realize this is very sudden. It doesn't give you much time to prepare, but for me it's necessary."

Chelsea got up from her chair and grabbed a toy, placing it inside a box. She looked forward to going to Paris with Sebastian, but the idea seemed easier to accept when she had a few weeks to prepare. Leaving in a few days made her feel anxious.

"Sebastian, please hear me when I say that I really do want to be with you in Paris. I don't have any doubts about that. I thought I'd have more time. I wanted to go shopping and take my time getting ready. This feels so rushed."

Sebastian sat back in his chair and nodded.

"I understand. I suppose there is another way. Maybe even a better option. I could go ahead and attend my meetings and get the house ready for your arrival. I had thought about doing that but wondered how you would feel traveling alone."

Chelsea laughed, "You don't have to worry about me. I can take care of myself. I love the idea."

She leaned down and kissed his cheek

"Thank you for being so understanding. Now, how would you like to help me with these gifts?"

Maggie finished writing in her journal and sat by the window watching the butterflies swarm the purple flowers. Her friend Rose always said that sitting in this chair inspired her to write. Rose introduced journaling to her and from that day forward Maggie made sure to carve out an hour in her day to write the words that wouldn't come any other way.

Sharing her feelings with others close to her helped to heal whatever needed attention in her life. But private time alone with her thoughts, although challenging at first, was now an essential part of her life and her peace of mind.

Breast cancer had become her muse—the inspiration for introspection and soul-searching. She had regrets, plenty of them in fact, but somehow their power diminished when she sat in this chair and contemplated what she would have done differently.

There wasn't much to change, even with Daniel's cheating and secret life. They had built a beautiful family and she had children and grandchildren that she was immensely proud of, and some of that credit had to go to her former husband.

Her cell phone buzzed.

"Hey, Chelsea, where are you?"

"I'm headed your way. I've spent the morning at Sebastian's wrapping gifts. I brought everything over there so the kids can't see what I'm doing."

"Very smart. Lily won't snoop, but Olivia, I'm not so sure."

"Listen, I'm starving and have a craving for Mexican food. Care to join me at Cantina Captiva for a margarita and burrito?"

"I haven't eaten there in months. I'm ready for lunch so that sounds like a good idea to me. Let me tell Paolo and I'll meet you there in fifteen minutes."

Maggie placed her leather-bound journal among her books and ran to the carriage house to find Paolo and apply a bit of makeup. The restaurant wasn't far from the inn, so she walked down Andy Rosse Lane waving to friends and business owners as she passed.

Chelsea was already waiting for her at the front door when she arrived.

"I don't think I'll ever get used to a Christmas without snow. I love all the decorations I saw walking here, but Christmas lights wrapped around palm trees will never replace a white Christmas."

Chelsea laughed. "I know what you mean. It took Carl and me a while to get used to it too."

They went inside and found a table toward the back of the room. It was early and there weren't many customers for lunch. They ordered a pitcher of margaritas and then looked over the menu.

"I'm glad you called to have lunch. You've been on my mind."

"You mean more than usual?"

"Very funny. With everything that's been going on, I haven't had an opportunity to talk with you privately."

"Maggie, whatever it is, I think you should wait for the margaritas. You've got drama written all over your face. Who is it this time? I already know about Lauren, and Sarah seems to be doing well. Let me guess, are Christopher and Becca having trouble?"

Maggie didn't know any other way to say it, so she blurted it out.

"I'm afraid this time it's me. I've got breast cancer."

"Oh Maggie…"

Chelsea reached across the table and took Maggie's hand.

The waiter came with the pitcher and two glasses. He poured their drinks and took their food order. As soon as he left, Chelsea took several long gulps of her margarita.

"I should have told you sooner, but with Lauren and the festival, there wasn't a good time to tell you. Even now, I can't believe I'm saying these words."

"Tell me everything the doctor said. Do you know what stage it is?"

"I think I'm lucky that they caught it when they did. It's in its very early stages. They're giving me an option of lumpectomy or mastectomy, but they're leaning toward the mastectomy because even though the cancer hasn't spread, it's a large area. A lumpectomy might not get it all."

"What are you going to do?"

Maggie took several sips of her drink before answering.

"Before I make that decision, I'm going to get a second opinion."

"I'm glad to hear you say that. Do you have a doctor in mind? If you don't, I highly recommend Carl's oncologist. He was wonderful."

"Thank you, Chelsea. If you could help me get an appointment as quickly as possible with him, I'd be grateful. This time of year, it's hard to schedule things. As much as I'm looking forward to the holiday and spending it with my children, Christmas is getting in the way of dealing with this quickly."

"I guess I understand why everyone was so willing to change their plans and come down to Captiva for Christmas."

Maggie shook her head.

"I haven't told them."

"What?"

Chelsea's voice filled the room, and so she lowered it to a whisper.

"I'm sorry but what? Why haven't you told them?"

"It's just not the kind of thing that I want to drop on them on the phone. I'm going to tell everyone when they're here for Christmas. My mother is coming too, so everyone will know. The only thing is I want to wait until after the kids have gone to bed on Christmas Eve. I don't want them in the room when I tell my kids. The children won't understand anyway, and besides, waiting for Santa is a pretty big motivator to get them off to sleep as early as possible."

Chelsea nodded. "Sounds like a good idea. I'm going to be with you when you tell them. Sebastian is leaving in two days. He has a meeting on the 28th and wants to get the house ready. I'm supposed to fly there after New Year's but I'm not going."

"Why not?"

"I'm not leaving my best friend in the world when she's going to need me. I want to be here for you. Paris will always be there. I can go in a few months after you're better."

Maggie didn't hold back her anger.

"No way. You are getting on that plane if I have to drag you there. If you're not leaving until New Year's then you'll be here for me when I get the second opinion. As far as the surgery and chemo or radiation, Paolo and Sarah are here. It's not like I won't have people around me who can help. You need to go to Paris."

Chelsea looked sad, as if Maggie had hurt her feelings.

"Chelsea, you are my best friend and I love you, but I won't get through this knowing that you stayed here instead of going to Paris. If you love me then do this for me. I need to know that for once in your life you are thinking of yourself instead of everyone else. It's what Carl would want for you."

Maggie tried to remember the last time she saw tears in Chelsea's eyes. Her strong and determined friend overcame many difficulties in her life and had always held her head up high during those times. Now, sitting across from her, Maggie could see the tears and she fought not to let the sight turn their lunch into a crying scene.

Chelsea nodded. "Promise me that you'll call me and keep me updated every step of the way."

"I promise."

Chelsea looked Maggie in the eye. "I'm serious, if you need me, I want you to tell me. Don't you dare hold back. Promise?"

"I won't hold back."

Chelsea filled her glass for the second time.

"You're going to beat this, you know. We're going to look back on this day and laugh at how much we drank."

"Chelsea, I've only had one glass."

"Oh, you're right. I guess I'll look back on this day and remember how much I drank. Do you mind if I order us another pitcher?"

Maggie smiled at her. She could tell that Chelsea already was suffering the effects of the alcohol.

"I think maybe you've had enough."

Their food came and just in time too, Maggie thought. She'd have to drive Chelsea's car to her house and walk back to the inn from there. It was a good thing that Lauren and the girls had gone to Cape Coral for the day.

She remembered the first time Chelsea created the inn's signature drink, the Key Limetini. She'd had far too much to drink that day as well. It was the first time Maggie had ever heard Chelsea snore. Something told her that it might be a good idea to ask Lauren to stop over for a visit when she returned. No point in frightening Olivia and Lily with scary and unusual sounds coming from Chelsea's bedroom.

CHAPTER 18

*a*fter lunch, Chelsea didn't go back to her house instead opting to sit with Maggie on the porch swing. Other than the occasional cold and flu, Maggie had never been sick a day in her life. When she was run down, Daniel wasn't the type to fuss over her or help around the house, and so, Chelsea hovering confused her.

"Are you going to be like this until you leave for Paris?"

"Like what?"

"Like I'm this fragile person who needs watching 24/7."

"I'm sorry, Maggie. I'm still processing."

Maggie's cell phone buzzed, and Beth's name appeared. She answered the call and put her on speaker.

"Hi, honey. Chelsea and I are sitting on the porch. I've put you on speaker. How is everything up there?"

"Hey, Mom. Hi Chelsea. I'm sorry to bother you with this but we've been able to get flights for everyone so that's the good news. The bad news is that we can't get a reservation anywhere. I tried all the hotels and even looked at renting a house, but everything is booked. I'm not surprised since it's Christmas, but I don't know what to tell you. I guess we could get a place off-island, but that would be a pain."

"Oh dear. I'd hoped that wouldn't be an issue. It's only two nights, you guys are all coming to the inn on the 23rd so maybe off-island is necessary. I know it's not ideal, but it's better than nothing."

Chelsea interrupted them.

"Wait. I think I've got a solution. Why not stay at Sebastian's? I don't think his kids would mind because he isn't even going to be here for Christmas so why should they care?"

Maggie was elated.

"Oh, Chelsea what a great idea. I hope he won't mind. It is only for two nights so it shouldn't be much of a bother."

"I'm sure it will be fine. Don't you worry, Beth. You all come along, and I'll get the place ready for you. We can't wait to see you."

"Thanks, Chelsea, and please thank Sebastian for us."

"Will do."

"Oh wait. Mom, before I go, I wanted to let you know that I got in touch with Grandma and she's coming with us."

"That makes three phone calls to grandma. I already called her and then I found out that Michael called her too. Didn't she ever mention our calls to her?"

"Nope. She never said a word."

"Typical. She loves all the attention. Thanks for looking after her when you fly down. I know she can be a handful, but she loves you all. It will be good to have everyone here for Christmas, even Grandma."

Beth laughed at that comment.

"We'll see you soon. Bye Chelsea."

"Bye honey. Love you."

Maggie ended the call and turned to Chelsea.

"Thank you so much for this. I know you're probably sorry

not to spend the holiday with Sebastian, but something good did come out of it. Are you sure he won't mind?"

"Absolutely. I should get going. I'll call him as soon as I get home. As far as Paris goes, I'm fine with him not being here for the holidays. I know we'll have lots of time to be together in Paris but right now all I want to do is be an unofficial Wheeler, at least for Christmas."

Maggie put her arm around her friend.

"It wouldn't be Christmas without you, Chelsea. You are family. Don't you ever forget it."

They stayed on the porch swing for another hour. Maggie was glad that she'd confided in Chelsea. As difficult as it was to think about the cancer, with her family and dearest friend's support, she knew she'd be able to withstand whatever was thrown in her path. She wasn't alone and for that she was immensely grateful.

"Probation? What do you mean probation? This guy has been abusing his wife for months now."

"I understand Ms. Hutchins, but he's never been arrested for it before. In the court's eyes, this is his first offense."

"That's ridiculous. You know that women often don't press charges, that's not the case this time. His wife wants him in jail."

Sarah could see Ciara talking to someone in the hall. She waved her hand motioning for her to come into the office.

"What does his wife need to do to make that happen?"

"Nothing at this point. My advice is to file a restraining order and stay as far away from him as possible."

"Officer Mendon, she already has a restraining order against him. How is it that you don't know that already?"

Sarah didn't wait for the man to respond, instead, she hung up and threw her cell phone onto the desk.

"Willy is out of jail. They have him on probation. That terrible

ANNIE CABOT

person is walking around the streets, and you can just bet he'll try to contact Hope."

Ciara ran her hand through her hair. "We can't let that happen. I have to assume that Hope already knows?"

Sarah nodded. "Police contacted her before he called me. She's got to be terrified."

"I think we better get over to the shelter and talk to her. Hopefully, he hasn't tried to contact her."

"If he does, that would break the rules of his probation and the restraining order. He's too sneaky for that. If I had to guess, he'll sweet talk her. Threatening her will get him arrested again. No, he won't do it that way. He'll be Prince Charming."

Sarah grabbed her handbag and started for the door but froze in place. Ciara turned to see what had stopped her and found Willy McKenna standing in front of them, a gun pointed in Sarah's direction.

"Sarah Hutchins, I believe I have you to thank for brainwashing my wife. It's because of you that she left me."

Sarah's heart beat fast in her chest and she moved her hand to her unborn child.

"No, Willy. It's because of you that she left. You can't keep beating on a woman and think she'll love you for it. Hope doesn't deserve how you've been treating her."

Sarah kept looking at Ciara for any sign of what to do. Terrified, both women tried to remain calm and not provoke him.

"You both need to sit down. I don't want either of you thinking you can run at me or try to leave the room."

Sarah and Ciara slowly moved to their chairs and sat. Sarah kept talking in hopes she could reason with him.

"Willy, right now you can walk out of here and try to start a new life. You don't have to do this."

"Right. Like they're going to let me walk off into the sunset after this."

Ciara spoke next.

"What exactly is your plan? Are you here to scare us? Is there something that you want?"

He walked into the office and kept his voice low.

"One of two things is going to happen. Either Ms. Hutchins places a call to Hope to tell her she wants to talk to her and ask her to come here, or I'm going to shoot Ms. Hutchins."

Ciara looked at Sarah. Her face made it clear which choice she wanted Sarah to make, but Sarah had other ideas.

"I'm not going to call Hope, Willy. She's happy now. Let her be."

Sarah knew Ciara didn't approve of her choice, but she couldn't see herself being responsible for Hope's death.

Ciara's ashen face stared at her. "Sarah, you have no choice. Call her."

Sarah struggled with her choice, placing her hand on her belly. She didn't want to die but more than that she needed to protect her child. She picked up her cell phone and squeezed it, her knuckles white from the pressure. The choice was taken from her when Hope walked into the office.

"I'm here, Willy."

Willy turned to look at his wife and he started to cry.

"Oh, baby, I'm so glad you came. I was so worried about you."

He walked toward Hope but she moved back and away from him.

"Hope, you don't have to be afraid of me. Why are you afraid of me? You know I love you."

"You don't love me, Willy. You think beating me is love? You have no idea what love is. I'm not going back with you no matter what."

Willy turned to look at Ciara and Sarah.

"You see what you've done? You've turned my wife against me."

Turning back to Hope, he motioned for her to walk to the other side of the room to join Sarah and Ciara. He seemed nervous and unsure of what to do next. They could hear police sirens getting louder as they approached the building. Hope did what she could to convince Willy to give himself up.

"The cops called me and told me you were out on probation. I was coming to Sarah's office to talk to her and Ms. Moretti about you. I called the police the minute I saw your truck outside. It's no use, Willy. You have to give yourself up."

It seemed like an hour since Willy walked into her office but in truth it was less than fifteen minutes. Now, with the police outside Sarah worried Willy might get desperate. She didn't have to wonder for long. He walked toward them and grabbed Hope, pointing the gun at her head. Walking back toward the door, he ordered her and Ciara to stay in their chairs.

"I'm walking out of here with my wife. If they shoot me they shoot her. As far as I'm concerned that's fine with me. I'm not living without her one way or the other."

Once out of their sight, Sarah knew where Willy was headed.

"He's going out the back way."

They got up from their chairs and slowly walked to the door. Peering out and looking left they saw Willy running to the back, Hope still in his grips.

Within seconds gunfire erupted and Sarah began to pray.

"Dear, God. Please. Let her be ok."

Several police officers came running inside and Sarah suddenly felt weak. Her legs gave out from under her.

"Sarah!"

Ciara caught her and they both fell to the floor. Two officers came to help, and one called for the EMT to enter the building. Sarah was still conscious and could see activity around her.

"Is he dead?"

"He is."

"Hope?"

"She's fine."

That was the last thing Sarah remembered.

CHAPTER 19

*A*fter Maggie got the call from Trevor, she and Paolo raced to the hospital. Trevor found out from Ciara who was with Sarah in the emergency room.

Maggie was too shaken to drive so Paolo got behind the wheel.

"Maggie, exactly what did Trevor say?"

"He said there was a hostage situation at the Outreach Center. It seems that the husband of a woman Sarah helped had a gun and confronted Sarah and Ciara in Sarah's office. He said that Sarah is going to be ok but because of the baby, they want to keep her at the hospital overnight."

"What about Ciara? Is she ok?"

"Yes. He said that they're both fine."

"What about the guy? Did they arrest him?"

Maggie shook her head.

"No. He's dead. His wife showed up and he held a gun to her head. I don't know how they did it but the police were able to shoot him. Thank God Sarah and Ciara are all right."

Paolo's driving got them to the hospital in record time. They found a parking spot close to the emergency room. Running inside they saw Ciara in the corner of the room on her cell phone.

"Where is she?"

Ciara ended her call and ran to her brother.

"Are you all right?"

"I'm fine, Paolo, and Sarah is going to be all right. They just need to keep her here for observation. Come with me."

Ciara directed them down the hall and into the room where Sarah lay. Trevor stood by the bed.

"Mom!"

Maggie leaned over the bed railing and hugged Sarah. She noticed fluids going into a line in Sarah's arm. A taped needle on her right arm worried Maggie.

"What's this?"

"It's nothing. I guess I was dehydrated, so they decided to give me fluids. I'm ok and the baby is doing well. No need to worry. I'm so sorry to scare you like this."

"Honey don't be silly; this wasn't your fault."

The television overhead showed a news reporter in front of the Outreach Center.

"Sarah, what in the world happened?"

"I'll tell you what happened. If the judge had done his job and put Willy behind bars, none of this would have happened. He'd been abusing his wife for months and nothing was done about it. When he finally got arrested, they let him out on probation. He wasted no time in getting his revenge."

"He first went to the shelter, but security wouldn't let him in. We're still trying to track down why that security officer didn't report the incident. In the meantime, he knew where to find us, and so that was his next move." Ciara said.

Sarah nodded. "He wanted us to call his wife and get her to come over to the center. We didn't have to. Hope showed up and Willy took her hostage. He went out the back door. That's the last time we saw him. The next thing we heard was gun shots outside. I guess that's when I passed out."

"I think you need to take a break from that job, at least for the rest of the pregnancy," Maggie insisted.

Sarah shook her head.

"No. I can't let this one incident scare me. What do they call it — getting back on the horse?"

"Sarah, this job has its dangers. You're dealing with people who are only thinking about themselves. They're not going to worry about your safety or health."

"Seriously? How can you say that? These people are victims because they thought of everyone else BUT themselves. If we don't help them, no one will. The people I work with are dedicated and compassionate individuals who want to help others who are in need and can't help themselves. This job is very important to me, Mom, and I intend on continuing this work."

Maggie looked at Trevor for support.

"Trevor, what do you think?"

Trevor took Sarah's hand and answered.

"Have you ever been successful trying to stop Sarah from doing something she's passionate about?"

Maggie knew what he meant. Sarah was as strong-willed and determined as the rest of her children.

Trevor smiled at Sarah.

"The truth is that I'm incredibly proud of her. She's an amazing example for our children."

Paolo put his arm around Ciara.

"I know what you mean, Trevor. I feel the same way about my sister."

A doctor pushed aside the curtain and joined the group.

"I see you've got quite a large support system. I hate to bother you Sarah, but there are a couple of police officers who would like to talk with you. I've told them to go get a cup of coffee and come back in about thirty minutes. Take a few minutes with your family and then we're going to move you upstairs to the maternity ward just for the night. The police can talk with you there. How does that sound?"

"Thank you, doctor."

As he left the room, Sarah made her announcement.

"As soon as I get out of here tomorrow, Ciara and I have some work to do. We've got to get the kitchen ready for the Christmas soup kitchen and then we've got the dinner and Christmas party at the shelter. Lots to do in the next two days."

Maggie shrugged and sighed.

"I give up. Will you at least promise me to sit down and rest if you get tired?"

Maggie looked at Ciara.

"You'll watch over her, right?"

"Of course, Maggie. I won't let her out of my sight."

"Noah and I are going to be there too. I want him to see first-hand what it means to care for others. He's going to hand out the Christmas cookies and soda. He can't wait. The nanny will watch Sophia while we're there."

He looked at Maggie.

"I promise we'll all look after her."

Maggie nodded.

"Make sure you don't forget about us. The family will be here tomorrow afternoon. I expect to spend the rest of the day today fielding calls from everyone asking about you."

Sarah smiled.

"Tell them their sister is a tough one, and that I'll see them in a couple of days."

Maggie kissed Sarah's head.

"Something tells me that your brothers and sisters know how tough you are. Just once, I'd like you to admit you're not superhuman."

Sarah laughed at that, and then pointed a finger at her mother.

"You first."

Chelsea looked out beyond the lanai and watched the ocean waves crash against the sand. Glad to spend the morning with Sebastian, she did her best to hide her disappointment at his leaving. They'd see each other again in a few weeks, but his absence during the holidays suddenly made her feel sad.

As usual, she didn't let her feelings be known and turned to look at him with a cheerful expression.

"You're going to miss this view."

Sebastian teased her.

"You mean I won't be happy looking at the Eiffel Tower?"

"Oh, that little thing? Doesn't hold a candle to the glorious sounds and sights of Captiva Island. I guess you'll just have to suffer until you're back here."

"I'll tell you why I'll suffer. Until I see you again, I'm going to be the most miserable man in all of France."

Chelsea leaned down and kissed him on the lips.

"Good, that's your punishment for leaving me at Christmas."

Their playful exchange was the norm for them, and Chelsea kept the light banter going so that he wouldn't suspect her pain. As sad as she was to see him go, Chelsea had so much to focus on during the holidays, the next few weeks would fly by.

"How have your children reacted to you not being here for Christmas?"

Sebastian shrugged.

"They're used to me taking off at the worst times. Ever since they were little, I was always missing at the most inopportune times. I think they inherited my lifestyle. None of them are married and travel all the time. Jordan will be in Ireland for the holidays and the other two are off on cruises. No one is going to miss me; I can promise you that."

Chelsea couldn't understand Sebastian's family. They seemed disconnected and without affection. She wondered whether they were like that when his wife was alive or if it was a consequence of her accident that pulled them apart. Either way, it seemed tragic to her.

When the doorbell rang, Chelsea opened the front door.

"Airport limo for Mr. Barlowe."

"Yes, he'll be right there. You can take his luggage."

Sebastian wheeled out the front door. The driver helped him into the handicapped van. Chelsea watched him as the chair elevated to a leveled spot before it turned and moved him further into the limo.

She stepped inside briefly to give him one last kiss.

"Don't go chasing all those Parisian women."

"Chelsea, I don't think it's possible for me to chase anyone."

"Ok, then, don't let them chase you. Got it?"

"I've got it."

She found it impossible to keep her eyes from watering, and so she gave in and let him see how much his leaving affected her.

"I love you, Sebastian. I thought you should know."

"I love you, too. See you in a few weeks."

The door closed and Chelsea turned to walk back inside when the window of the van lowered.

"Chelsea!"

She turned to look at him.

"Merry Christmas, my love."

"Merry Christmas, Sebastian."

CHAPTER 20

*M*aggie and Paolo returned to the inn and waved to their guests who were enjoying afternoon tea under the grapevine trellis. The stress of the morning gave her a headache and the pounding at her temples sought the smells and sounds of the ocean.

Paolo decided to drive to Sanibellia to handle some business paperwork, and Maggie thought it a great opportunity to spend the afternoon at the beach. She changed into her swimsuit, filled her beach bag with suntan lotion, a towel, her journal, a bottle of water and an apple, and made her way down to her favorite private spot on the sand, carrying her backpack-styled beach chair.

She wasted no time diving into the water. When she surfaced, she turned and let her body go limp. Floating along with the waves, she smiled thinking how no medication could heal her stress better than the feel of the salt water against her skin.

Several tourists stood at the edge of the sea holding their cell phones and cameras up. She turned to look at what they were filming and saw two dolphins playing behind her. They dove back under and were very close. She'd seen dolphins several times but had never been this close to them.

Something kept her from getting out of the water. She felt mesmerized by the marine mammals and continued to float near them. Maggie felt like she and the dolphins were the only creatures in the water, and indeed she was right. She swam closer to the shore to help her feet touch the ground, and found that other than the dolphins, she was alone in the water.

She wasn't scared. The dolphins didn't approach her, and she continued to float, hearing the pulsing of her heart beating in her ears. This was her paradise, her oasis from everything that frightened and worried her. The dolphins seemed to understand how special the sea was to her as much as it was to them, and for a few moments shared the lapping water in a dance.

When she tired, she went back to her chair and dried off. She watched Finn and Joshua Powell take beachgoers out parasailing. Their sister, Becca would soon join them to celebrate Christmas, and Christopher would be back with her for the holiday. Maggie loved how Becca and Christopher got along so well, and that both families supported their relationship. She wondered how long before Christopher proposed to Becca.

Her cell phone buzzed and although she didn't recognize the number, decided to answer.

"Hello?"

"Hello, Ms. Moretti, this is Emily's mother, Evelyn. I know this is rather awkward, but I wanted to talk to you about my daughter."

Maggie thought that a phone call from Evelyn years ago would have been described as awkward, but now, Maggie was curious why Evelyn felt she needed to talk with her lover's wife. Although not angry, Maggie didn't feel she needed to be polite.

"What can I do for you?"

"Emily plans to visit Captiva with her half-siblings tomorrow.

Even though I don't approve, I have little say about it given the fact that she is over eighteen and can afford to pay for it herself."

Her last statement didn't go unnoticed by Maggie considering that Daniel had left one hundred thousand dollars to Emily in his hidden-from-his-wife-will.

"Then why are you calling?"

There was a hesitation on the other end of the line.

"Ms. Moretti, I can't say that I wish my relationship with Daniel didn't happen, because if I did, then I wouldn't have my daughter, whom I love more than anything in this world. But, it was a long time ago, and I've learned a thing or two along the way. Even though I want to apologize to you, that's not the reason for the call."

Maggie waited and said nothing.

"I understand that you've never met Emily."

"That's right."

"I don't believe Emily would have shared with your family that she is autistic. It's not something she would feel comfortable talking about, or able to explain for that matter."

Maggie was surprised to hear this. No one had ever said a word to her about Emily being autistic.

"I don't know if Emily told them, but no one has mentioned it to me."

"You might not notice it at first, but if you and your family spend any length of time with her, you'll see that she's a little different. She might get overwhelmed in social situations, or you might see her having repetitive behaviors. She can have difficulty with communication and understanding nuanced dialogue will be a problem."

"I'm glad you told me. I'll make my children aware. I have to admit, I don't know much about autism, but I do know there is a spectrum."

"If you don't mind, I'd like to send you an email with more in-depth detail about her diagnosis as a teenager. It's taken many years for me to learn how to communicate with her and it's not something you will grasp overnight. All I wanted was to make you aware that if she is overwhelmed with noises or sounds she may need to seek a quiet place that is her own."

"Do you think Emily's coming here is a mistake?"

"Emily's desire to be with her brothers and sisters is something I've worried about. You have a large family and I've struggled with her meeting everyone at the same time. I must say the way your children have accepted her warms my heart and gives me hope that she'll have family to be with if anything should happen to me. I love my daughter and worry about her when she does anything on her own, but I can't hover or be with her all the time. It doesn't stop me from worrying."

"I think I'd feel the same."

Another pause made the conversation uncomfortable, so Maggie extended a kindness.

"I'm looking forward to meeting Emily. From what my children tell me, she's a lovely young woman. I'm sure you are the reason for that."

"Daniel wasn't in her life as much as I wanted him to be for obvious reasons, but he did love Emily. Forgive me for saying this but I worried that you might harbor some anger toward me and therefore toward Emily."

"You needn't worry about that Evelyn. Emily will always be welcome in our home and with her siblings. What happened between you and Daniel was a long time ago and I've made peace with that and many other things. Emily will feel welcomed, I can promise you that."

"Thank you. Even if she won't be with me, I'm glad she'll be with family for Christmas. I won't keep you any longer. You now have my cell phone number. I'd appreciate it if you'd let me know either by text or a call if there are any problems, or if you have any questions. Please don't let Emily know that I've called you, but I think it's important that you share what I've told you with the rest of the family."

"Of course. Anything we can do to make this visit a success for Emily we'll certainly do. Please send whatever information you have to help us all better understand. If Emily is going to be a part of this family, we want her to feel safe when she is with us."

"Thank you for being so understanding. Goodbye, Ms. Moretti and Merry Christmas."

"Evelyn, please call me Maggie, and Merry Christmas to you, too."

Beth stood near the gate and waited for Emily and Gabriel to get their bagels and orange juice. Everyone else had found a seat waiting to board the fully booked flight.

Emily was already eating her bagel when they returned to the gate. Gabriel motioned to a few empty seats next to the rest of the family.

"Sorry. I didn't think the line would be so long."

"No problem. I knew you'd be wanting something to eat before we boarded the plane. You haven't eaten anything in two hours, you must be starving."

"Why do you always make fun of my appetite?"

Emily laughed at their exchange.

"Does she really always make fun of you?"

"Don't listen to him, Emily. He just wants you to feel sorry for him."

Beth's grandmother shook her head.

"I don't understand why everyone has to buy their food on the go. Why not make something at home that you can take with you? All these coffee shops and sandwich places. No wonder people don't have any money in the bank."

"Grandma, with the amount of food that Gabriel eats, I'd be in the kitchen all day long."

"What's wrong with that? If it was good enough for me, it should be good enough for you."

Gabriel smiled at Beth.

"I love your grandmother."

Michael overheard the conversation.

"I agree with grandma. Brea is always making me something to eat. I take my lunch every day."

Beth looked at Brea and frowned.

"Please tell me he's joking?"

"I'd say he's not joking but he certainly is exaggerating. He takes his lunch sometimes, not always."

Christopher interrupted them.

"Um, if you guys were paying attention, you'd notice that we're boarding. Becca and I are getting in line to get on first. See you guys in Florida."

"Come on, grandma. Let's get in line."

"I'm coming. There's not much use in rushing me. I've only got one speed, and that's slow."

Maggie stood at the window looking down at the driveway. Paolo fussed with the tv remote trying to get his football game to come on.

"There's no use in looking out that window, they won't get here any faster."

"Oh, hush. I don't care, I can barely stand the excitement."

Looking at her watch, she sighed.

"They should be here by now. The traffic getting on the island must be backed up."

Paolo tried to settle Maggie's nerves by distracting her.

"Why don't you make a cup of tea and relax? They'll get here when they get here."

"I don't want a cup of tea. By the way, don't think you're going to sit up here watching football all afternoon. When they get here you'd better turn that thing off."

She didn't really care if Paolo watched the game. She was so fidgety that she needed something to focus on and complaining about his sitting in front of the tv all afternoon was as good as anything else.

Paolo paid her no mind. He was already deep into the game when two vans pulled up outside.

"They're here! Paolo, come on."

Maggie didn't wait to see how long it would take him to turn the tv off. She was half-way down the stairs before she could hear him behind her.

Beth jumped out of the van, followed by Michael. She hugged Beth tight and pulled Michael to join them. The group hug grew, and Christopher walked toward her. His limp noticeably better than when she saw him last.

"My babies are back."

Becca smiled and approached her.

"Remember me?"

"You bet I do. Come here and give me a hug."

Brea followed Becca and Cora and Quinn ran to hug Maggie as well. It was Maggie's mother, Sarah who slowly walked toward her daughter.

"Hello, dear. You're looking thin. Are you eating enough?"

"Hello mother. Yes, I'm eating plenty. I've got two private chefs who will cook me anything I want at any time of the day. Don't you worry about me."

"That's all well and good, but you should watch what you're eating. You need some meat on your bones."

Emily stood back near the van and waited for someone to

introduce her. Maggie couldn't believe how much she looked like Beth.

"You must be Emily. I bet you've already heard how much you and Beth look so much alike. I swear the two of you could be twins. I'm so happy to meet you. We're a hugging family so I hope you don't mind if I give you a hug?"

Emily looked uncomfortable and Maggie wondered if hugging her was a mistake. Putting her arms around Emily, Maggie whispered, "You and I are going to be great friends."

Maggie couldn't tell if the hug was uncomfortable or if her words frightened the young woman, but whichever it was she would learn soon enough where the boundaries were.

Emily smiled and quickly pulled away.

"Thank you for having me."

Paolo hugged everyone and then they all turned and waved as Lauren, Chelsea, Olivia, and Lily drove toward them. Getting out of Chelsea's car, Lauren ran to Beth and threw her arms around her. She squeezed her sister tight. They stayed in that embrace for longer than usual and Maggie knew why.

Maggie thought back to when her children were young and always fighting. She'd remind them that one day they would need one another and wanted them to learn to get along. Countless situations proved her right. Regardless of whether a Code Red was called or not. Her children had always stepped up and done the right thing for each other. It made her proud to see Lauren and Beth hold each other in a comforting embrace.

Michael put his arm around Maggie.

"Tell us about Sarah. How is she doing?"

Maggie tapped his arm. "She's fine. Her and the baby were unharmed, but she fainted from dehydration, so they kept her in the hospital. You know Sarah, the minute she got out of bed she went right back to barking orders and working at the Outreach Center and Domestic Violence Shelter. I'm sure she and Trevor and the kids will be by sometime in the next day or two."

Christopher hugged Chelsea. "You're looking radiant Ms. Marsden, can I assume you're in love?"

"Oh, you. You can assume whatever you like, I'm not telling you a thing."

He laughed and then introduced Emily to her.

"I can tell you're a Wheeler. Those pretty blue eyes and freckles give you away."

Emily nodded and then looked down at the ground. Without being told of Emily's autism, Maggie might think there was something wrong, but she had read that certain social situations could be difficult. She stopped Chelsea from asking too many questions and put her hands together.

"Well, shall we drive over to Sebastian's house and get you all situated? It's not far from here."

Becca kissed Christopher and then took her backpack and carryon out of the van. She waved and yelled out to the group, "I'll catch up with you all later. I'm going over to visit with my father and brothers. You all have fun."

Paolo went back inside to watch his football game, and Maggie jumped into Chelsea's car. The others followed behind.

Maggie's prayers had been answered. All of her children would be together around the Christmas tree this year. She didn't want to look back or worry about the future. All Maggie wanted was to enjoy today—to take in every moment during the next few days and create memories that her children would hold in their hearts forever.

CHAPTER 21

$\mathcal{T}$he steady stream of people coming into the Outreach Center's soup kitchen worried Sarah. She looked down at the clipboard and tried to make sense of the numbers.

"Ciara, I think we're going to outpace last year's numbers. Have you looked at the line outside?"

Ciara pulled the ties of her apron around her waist.

"Yup. I'm not surprised. Our numbers for the weekly food pantry distribution have shot up as well. That's what happens during the holidays. I think more people are struggling during this time of year more than any other. Don't worry about the food though. We've got plenty. I made sure of it."

"You're a wonder, Ciara. Math was never my strong suit in school. You should have seen the number of hours my mother sat with me at the kitchen table going over my algebra homework. I swear I still cringe at the memory. It was painful."

Ciara laughed.

"Trevor and Noah are outside. Trevor's talking to someone he knows standing in line. He told me to tell you that he and Noah are ready to help out. I expected Trevor, but not Noah. I think it's sweet the way he wants to help hand out food to people."

Sarah felt proud of Noah. Her son had shown a particular interest in her work and how she had been able to help so many who needed it. His only conundrum was whether to be in construction like his dad or work alongside his mother at the Outreach Center when he got older. Considering he was coming up on seven years old, Sarah didn't concern herself with his dilemma. He'd probably pick several more careers before he finally found his place in the world. For now, she was grateful Noah had a heart of generosity.

"I told Trevor that he and Noah should stand at the end of the line so the two of them can hand out bottled water and cans of soda. I won't be able to stand the cuteness, so you know I'll be taking a bunch of pictures with my cell phone."

"I have no doubt. I've got to get more chairs, so I'll talk to you later. Have fun."

As Ciara walked out of the room, Trevor and Noah walked in.

"Hey, you two, are you ready to work? We sure can use your help."

Noah's face lit up and Sarah gave him a hug. Trevor kissed Sarah's cheek.

"We're ready. We just dropped Sophia off with your mother. Everyone says hello and they can't wait to see you. Did you know your half-sister Emily was coming down?"

Sarah nodded. "Yes, Beth told me. I only met her that first time when everyone else did but Beth especially spends the most amount of time with her. What did you think of her?"

"She seems shy I think. She didn't say much. She sure looks like a Wheeler though. She and Beth could be twins."

"I know. I'm surprised to hear you say she seems shy. I didn't get that impression when I first met her at all. Maybe she's nervous about meeting Mom. I mean it is an awkward situation. I give her credit for reaching out. She seems brave to me."

Trevor nodded. "I agree. So, where do you want us?"

Sarah walked them to the end of the line.

"Right here. You and Noah can hand out bottles of water or soda. You just have to ask them what they want. Think you guys can do that?"

Noah nodded. "I can do it, Mommy."

"Trevor?"

Trevor smiled and gave Sarah a salute.

"I'll do my best, ma'am."

Sarah saluted back and smiled at the two of them and decided to wait before taking their picture. She wanted to capture them in action. She left them to do their job and walked into the kitchen.

Since the Willy McKenna drama, Sarah hadn't had a conversation with Hope about that day. Hope had been the bigger victim in all of this and it troubled Sarah that she didn't know what to say to the woman. Sarah could see Hope in the kitchen with the others who prepared the food trays but stayed clear of her until they had a private moment to talk.

When the last of the food had been distributed many lingered at the soup kitchen enjoying the sounds of Christmas music, cookies and coffee. Trevor and Noah headed to Captiva to join the family and pick up Sophia before heading home, while Sarah and Ciara went to the shelter to watch Santa Claus hand out Christmas presents to the children.

Sarah loved seeing the faces of the children as one-by-one Santa called out their names. One of the volunteers played Christmas carols on the piano in the corner while everyone enjoyed the alcohol-free eggnog and punch bowls.

A tap on her shoulder, Sarah turned to see Hope holding two presents.

"It's nothing special, just a little gift to say thank you to you and Ms. Moretti."

Sarah motioned for Ciara to join them, and Hope handed her a present.

"Should we open them now or wait?"

"It's up to you. You can open them now if you want."

Sarah and Ciara peeled the wrapping paper off their gifts and opened the boxes. Inside were two handmade paperweights.

"I made them myself when we had ceramics class. I know it's not much but…"

"It's lovely, Hope. I can't wait to put it on my desk. I'm only sorry that I don't have anything for you."

Ciara agreed.

"I love mine. Thank you, Hope. This is very sweet of you."

Hope looked pleased with their reaction.

"I'm so sorry for what Willy put you both through. You didn't deserve what happened."

Sarah stopped her.

"No. Hope. It wasn't your fault. We run this kind of risk all the time. The shelter is a safe place for women. We're so glad that you are now free to live your life without being afraid all the time."

Hope smiled and her face lit up.

"Speaking of living my life. I've decided to go back to school to get my GED. I want to go to college too. I'm not sure how I'm going to make that happen, but for the first time I feel like anything is possible."

"Hope, that's fantastic. I know you'll get to college. I believe in you."

Ciara nodded.

"Sarah's right. You're a strong young woman. You'll make it happen."

Hope hugged Sarah and Ciara and then joined the others around the Christmas tree. Wrapping paper was everywhere and the children were already playing with their toys.

"We better pick up this mess. I'll get the trash barrel," Ciara said.

Sarah shook her head at the happy chaos. Soon she'd be with her family and would share in the same holiday mayhem as her children and nieces surrounded the Christmas tree at the Key Lime Garden Inn. Nothing made her happier than knowing she'd been able to share the true meaning of the holiday with others less fortunate.

She knew how blessed she was to have family waiting for her back home. But family had come to mean so much more to her this Christmas. Her family had grown by the hundreds, and she held that knowledge close to her heart and promised herself that she'd remember this feeling every day of the year for the rest of her life.

Her shoes off and feet elevated, Sarah marveled that she'd been able to accomplish everything on her list. Now, sitting in her living room with Noah and Sophia sleeping in their beds, she rocked in her chair and watched the lights twinkle on their Christmas tree.

Trevor joined Sarah and offered her a most precious and desired gift—a foot massage.

"How about you lay down on the sofa and I'll rub your feet?"

"Is this in place of a gift from you under the tree or is this just because you're being nice?"

He laughed at her and shook his head.

"It depends. Have you been good? If you've been good then there will be something under the tree. If not, then enjoy this foot rub because it's all you're going to get. Well, that, and a bag of coal."

Sarah didn't care what the conditions were. She'd take the

foot massage under any circumstance. She lay down on the sofa and rested her head on the pillow.

"My ankles thank you."

"I noticed they were getting a little swollen when we were handing out water bottles."

"Yeah, I've got to watch how much sodium I'm taking in. Speaking of water bottles, how did Noah do? He looked like he was in charge, and you were working for him."

Trevor laughed.

"That just about says it all. I was handing someone a can of soda and he said, 'Daddy, you didn't ask him what he wanted to drink.' I had to apologize to the guy and then asked him what he wanted. Noah was right, the guy wanted water not soda. That kid is going to run the world when he grows up."

"So, what happened when you were over at the inn? What's everyone doing?"

"Well, it seems all are settled in at Sebastian's house. Becca went over to stay with her family. Chelsea, Lauren, Olivia and Lily are still staying at Chelsea's house. The guests are leaving day after tomorrow, but Christopher was able to stay in his old room on the first floor because that room is free. Emily seems glued to Beth, and I'm not sure how Gabriel feels about that."

"What do you mean?"

"As I told you, she seems a bit out of place, but I think she's become so close to Beth that everywhere Beth goes, Emily goes, and I mean everywhere. When Beth leaves the room, Emily follows her. You'll see what I mean when we're all together."

"That poor girl. You know what it's like when you're the new family member. We can be loud and overbearing. Don't get me wrong. We all love each other tremendously, but you know how much we're in each other's lives. Some people might find that a bit smothering. I hope Emily doesn't feel that way."

Trevor's eyes grew wide.

"Hey, speaking of that, I've got a question for you. What exactly is a Code Red?"

"Where did you hear about that?"

"When I was over at the inn, I heard Chelsea say something to your mother about it. She said something like, 'looks like your Code Red alert worked.'"

Sarah quickly sat up and grabbed Trevor's arm.

"Are you sure you heard that? Tell me exactly what you heard."

Trevor shrugged.

"Chelsea said 'your Code Red alert worked', and your mother laughed and put her finger to her mouth, like she was telling Chelsea not to say anything."

"Was Lauren anywhere near them when they were talking?"

"As a matter of fact, she was in the same room. I didn't think much about it at the time, but now that you mention it, Lauren turned to look at them, but Olivia and Lily came running into the room and that was the end of it. What is this all about?"

Sarah did her best to explain the history of the Wheeler family Code Red alerts and how her mother used it this time to get everyone down to Captiva to support Lauren in her 'time of need' which Sarah correctly renamed, 'Maggie's Christmas wish.'

"If Lauren finds out, she'll hit the roof, and I'm not sure I want to watch that explosion. Trust me, you don't want to see it either."

CHAPTER 22

*L*auren had explained to her clients that she'd be out of the office until the new year. Nell was to handle any additional inquiries and but that wasn't a good enough deterrent to keep Callum Foster at bay, and so, after the fourth attempt by Callum to contact Lauren, she had no choice but to answer his call.

"Hello, Lauren. I hope I haven't caught you at a bad time. I just wanted to check in with you to see how you are. I've left messages at the office for you to call, but when you didn't return any of them, I wondered if I've done something wrong. Are you all right?"

Lauren knew she should have been firm in her discussions with Callum, but just like everything else in her life, she'd taken the easy and cowardly way out—she said nothing and ran away.

"Callum, I'm sorry but I should have explained. I'm in Florida with my family for Christmas. I'm sure if you need anything, Nell can work with you."

"No, it's nothing like that. I only worried that perhaps in my efforts to explain my feelings, I might have scared you off."

Thus far, Lauren had demonstrated more patience than most

would, but now his presumptive comments were getting on her nerves.

"My time away from the office has nothing to do with you, Callum. I'm enjoying a perfectly wonderful holiday with my family."

She knew that was stretching the truth, but she wanted him to go away.

"You did say you were in Florida, did you not?"

"Yes, what of it?"

"I only ask because when I was last in your office the other day, your husband was there. Nell introduced us."

Shocked that Jeff and Callum had met, Lauren felt a panic rise in her throat.

"Callum, I have to go but before I do, I want to be very clear with you as I should have been earlier. This is not a punishment in any way, but my agency will not represent you going forward. I think it best that you contact another agent to help you find your home. As far as my personal life goes, I'm going to ask you to move on and stay out of my business. I don't have to explain myself to you or justify my life with you. That's something I should have said to you before. Your comment that you'll be waiting for me if ever I'm free was inappropriate at best, but certainly unwelcome. I wish you the best, but please don't contact me again."

She ended the call with an abruptness that seemed necessary. Being polite didn't work, and as much as she knew she'd enjoyed the attention from Callum, she forgave herself for letting his charm control her thoughts. She was human after all. Something she'd need to come to terms with where Jeff was concerned.

She called Nell's cell phone.

"Hey, Lauren. How are you? How is warm and sunny Florida?"

"Hey, Nell. All's great down here. I'm sorry to bother you at home, but Callum Foster called me. He said that Jeff was in the office the other day. You never said anything to me about it, so I wondered what was that all about?"

"Oh, Lauren, I'm so sorry. I didn't know what to do. Jeff told me not to tell you that he was there. He made it sound like it had to do with Christmas and a surprise."

"Why was he there in the first place? What did he want?"

"I have no idea. He said he was looking for a receipt, so he went through your desk. Then he asked me if I had any messages or anything that you might need. He said he'd be talking to you so I shouldn't bother you with any of it. I handed the messages over to him. While he was there, Callum came in, so I introduced them to each other."

Lauren was beside herself.

"Anything else?"

"No. That was all I noticed. Come to think of it, I don't think he ever got what he came in for. He went through your desk, but he never walked away with anything from it. I hope I haven't spoiled your surprise."

"No. Don't worry about it. I won't let him know that we talked."

"Oh, thank you. The last thing I want to do is be a Christmas grinch. Is that all or do you need me to do anything?"

"No, thank you, Nell. I'm good. Merry Christmas to you and your family. I'm sure you and your fiancé will have a romantic one."

"That's what I asked Santa for, so I hope you're right. Merry Christmas to you and yours, Lauren. See you next year."

As soon as she hung up the phone Lauren began pacing the floor. Jeff hadn't returned her calls not even to check on the girls. Nothing was making sense to her, and she had no control over her fate. More than anything she wanted desperately to talk to her husband and if possible, save her marriage. She was certain that whatever was happening between them could be resolved one way or the other.

❄

No more hiding!

Lauren found Chelsea at the kitchen table, coloring Christmas trees and candy canes with Olivia and Lily.

"Chelsea, would you mind watching the girls while I run over to the inn?"

"Not at all. We're making Christmas pictures to give as presents to everyone. Is everything ok?"

"Yes, at least I think it will be."

She kissed Olivia and Lily.

"You girls be good and mind Aunt Chelsea. I won't be long."

Determined to talk things through with her family, Lauren power-walked to the carriage house in hopes of finding her mother. When she got there, no one but Paolo was around.

"Where is everybody?"

"Your mother went over to Sebastian's to have lunch with the kids. Want me to drive you over there?"

"Would you, Paolo? I'm sorry to bother you, but I really need to talk with my mother."

"It's no bother. Truck is right there. Let me wash my hands and I'll be right there."

Lauren got inside the truck and waited for Paolo. Her breath coming in deep pants as if she was a bull waiting for combat. All this time she had quietly hidden away from confrontation, but now she dared anyone to stop her from saying what was on her mind. She didn't mean to be intimidating so she tried to calm down when she noticed Paolo's tightened face.

"Everything all right with you?"

She took a deep breath and smiled.

"Yes, thanks. I'm fine. How are you doing, Paolo? Our crazy family must drive you nuts sometimes. We're all running around with one drama after another. I'm sure it can be overwhelming at times."

Paolo shrugged in his usual way.

"I don't let things bother me too much. If you let yourself get too worked up, you find it was a waste of time because the drama doesn't last, and you feel physically sick for nothing. Isn't that where 'this too shall pass' comes from?"

Lauren laughed at Paolo's comment.

"I guess we'd all be better if we looked at life that way."

Within minutes they arrived at Sebastian's house. Maggie's car and the two vans were parked outside. Lauren jumped out of the truck.

"Thanks, Paolo. I'll come back in Mom's car."

She watched him drive away and went up to the front door. It was unlocked, so she stepped inside the foyer and called out.

Beth came running to the front, followed by Michael, Christopher and Maggie.

"Hi honey. I'm glad you joined us. Are the girls with you?"

"No, they're back at Chelsea's. The three of them are coloring. Is everyone here? I'd like to talk if you all are willing to listen."

"Let me go upstairs and talk to Brea. She and the girls were planning on going to Chelsea's to make Christmas cookies."

Maggie answered. "We all were, well, not the boys. That was the plan."

Turning to Lauren, Michael asked, "Why don't I drive Quinn and Cora over to Chelsea's so they can get started on the cookies, and you all can join them as soon as we finish here?"

Lauren nodded.

"Good idea to have the girls with Chelsea. Jackson's too young to understand so that's no big deal. We can wait."

Maggie added, "I told Sarah to come over to Chelsea's with Noah and Sophia. Maybe I should ask Trevor to stay there too. That's too many kids for Chelsea to handle alone, don't you think?"

Brea came downstairs and had a better idea.

"Why don't I take the girls and Jackson while you all talk?

Emily, would you care to come with us? We're going to make Christmas cookies."

"Yes. I love cookies. I've never actually made any, but I think it would be fun."

Lauren appreciated everyone working to create a quiet and private space to talk. There was so much she needed to get off her shoulders and she didn't want to worry any of the children with important grown-up talk.

They waited for Sarah and Trevor to join them and, as soon as they arrived, went outside onto the expansive lanai overlooking the ocean. Lauren took a breath and ran her hand through her hair. She knew what she wanted to say but kept her desire to not hurt anyone's feelings front and center.

"I guess you all know the situation. I saw Jeff having lunch with another woman, but instead of confronting him and getting to the bottom of the situation, I ran away to Florida instead. I know that I should have talked to him, and at first, I didn't want to. I was stubborn and refused to deal with the situation."

Christopher spoke up.

"Michael and I wanted to go over there and punch Jeff in the nose. Just so you know."

Everyone looked at Christopher as if he'd told an inappropriate joke.

"What? We wanted to defend our sister—nothing wrong with that."

"I appreciate that you guys, but I don't think that would solve anything. Besides, we don't really know what's going on there and I think it's best we hold out until we know more."

She looked at Sarah and winked.

"Anyway, as I said, I was stubborn and angry and didn't want to talk to him. Someone in this room helped me to remember what was most important and regain perspective. I decided to reach out to Jeff. The problem is he won't talk to me. I've tried to call him, and I've texted him several times with no answer. My mind is spinning and imagining all kinds of things. I don't know what to do. Most of all my heart breaks that the girls won't see their father on Christmas."

No one seemed to know what to do and so, Beth shrugged and looked at Maggie.

"No one calls a Code Red without a plan. We can't just sit here and not come up with some way to help Lauren."

Lauren looked at Maggie who tried to avoid eye contact with her.

"Mom! You called a Code Red?"

Maggie looked at Lauren and grimaced.

"Well, I had to do something. You needed the family around you for support."

"I don't believe this. You asked everyone to come down here for Christmas before you knew anything about Jeff and my issues. My leaving him and coming here turned out to be fortuitous. You used my situation to convince everyone that I needed them. That was the excuse you used to upend everyone's Christmas."

"Lauren, you are overreacting. There was no devious plot here. Is it a crime to want my family together for Christmas?"

"Mom, I thought everyone wanted to be on Captiva for Christmas because it was their wish—their choice. Now I find out that you manipulated my situation for your own selfish reasons. You really think I couldn't handle this on my own?"

"Lauren, I never said that. It's just that this family is stronger when we're all together, you know that."

Having slept late, Maggie's mother slowly walked down the stairs and joined the group.

"What's all the commotion? A person can't get a minute of sleep with all this racket. I thought we were going to make Christmas cookies over at Chelsea's today. What time are we leaving?"

No one said a word and Lauren suddenly wished she had

another method of transportation back to Chelsea's house. As it was, she would have to get in someone else's vehicle if she wasn't going to ride back with her mother.

Beth took Gabriel's hand and slowly walked to the front door.

"I feel like I've ruined Christmas with my big mouth. Christmas cookie-making is going to be a real blast. I think I'd rather have a root canal."

"You didn't ruin Christmas. Everything will work out."

Beth joined her grandmother and Lauren and got into a van with Sarah, Michael and Trevor. Christopher and Gabriel stayed back at Sebastian's, and Maggie drove back alone.

Fuming, Lauren was too angry to speak, and Sarah, Michael and Trevor were afraid to say anything so the four of them sat in silence. When they reached Chelsea's house, Sarah, Beth, and Lauren got out of the van without saying a word.

Trevor ran upstairs to get the keys from Brea for the parked van. He came back and hopped into the van and headed back to Sebastian's house.

Michael called out to Lauren as the women climbed the front stairs.

"The guys and I will pick you all up at five o'clock. There are too many of you to walk back to Sebastian's. Have fun."

Lauren didn't appreciate Michael's sarcastic comment and could see the smirk he barely tried to hide. The women walked up the stairs without speaking. Lauren didn't bother to explain the problem to her grandmother who would only add fuel to the fire with some inappropriate albeit wise statement.

However the next few hours went, Lauren's focus had shifted from her marriage problems to her mother's meddling in the blink of an eye. Because of this, she had no idea how the day would end, but predicting it would later prove humorous and shocking at the same time.

CHAPTER 23

*I*t began innocently enough. As the women talked, Lauren's voice tinged with sarcasm and insults. Mostly pointed at Beth, Maggie noticed the tension escalating among everyone but her grandchildren, Brea, Chelsea and Emily.

Knowing how confusing the situation must be for the newcomer, Maggie tried to steer all conversations toward the children and Emily.

"Emily, your gingerbread house cookie is adorable. Are you sure you've never done this before?"

As innocent as she could be, Emily tried to convince Maggie that this was her first time.

"Honest, Maggie. I've never done this before. I like it though."

"Quinn, that is the best Christmas tree cookie I've ever seen. Look at your ornaments. You've lined them up perfectly."

"Thanks, Grandma."

Cora, Olivia and Lily, not to be outdone, insisted their grandmother critique their creations as well.

"Oh, Olivia, I love that Santa Claus, and Lily and Cora's reindeers are perfect too. I can't wait to eat them all. You know, when my girls were little we always made Christmas cookies just like we're doing today."

Lauren had a response to that.

"Yes, that was back in the day when you could trust what was being said to you."

Beth didn't let that slide.

"I remember those days. I worked really hard to be as perfect as my big sisters, but I never seemed to make my Christmas cookies as perfect as theirs."

Although no one said anything for the next few moments, eyeballs moved from side to side watching each other and waiting for the next outburst.

Maggie realized that Brea and Chelsea had no idea what was going on, and there wasn't any time to bring them up to speed. All she could do was play referee and hope the Christmas cookie-making afternoon would soon be over. She hoped her girls would calm down and see how silly the whole thing was. Her wish turned out to be too much to hope for.

"Beth, I just rolled that dough out for my cookies. I didn't roll it out so you could jump right in with your cookie-cutter and hog the whole thing."

"I thought we were all using whatever cookie dough was available. I didn't think this was your cookie dough. Fine. I'll roll out another batch. You don't have to be so selfish."

And with that, Beth threw a small handful of flour Lauren's way.

"Oh, real mature, Beth."

A dusting of extra flour landed on Beth's apron and Lauren smiled, pleased with her aim.

Sarah stayed clear of the ensuing ruckus, thinking it best to protect her unborn child from the food fight that was about to start. However controlled Emily had been thus far, what she saw transpire between her sisters made her laugh and grab a handful of flour and dropping it on Chelsea's head.

It was a shocking move considering that Emily didn't have a clue what the whole fight was about in the first place. Knowing what she did about Emily's autism, Maggie didn't dare act angry or disappointed in any way. Instead, Maggie decided it best to approve and encourage Emily's actions. She did that by laughing at Chelsea's situation, and in doing so received just enough flour from her best friend to shut her up.

Brea did her best to keep the children from joining in the fun, but it was no use. Thankfully, Jackson and Sophia were sleeping upstairs. Quinn, Cora, Olivia and Lily didn't target each other, thinking it funnier to hit the adults instead. Before long, several of the women were on the kitchen floor laughing so hard they had to be careful they didn't inhale any of the flour hovering in the air.

It wasn't until Olivia and Lily ran to the front door, yelling for their father that the room went quiet, and the women sat completely still.

"Daddy! Look, we're making Christmas cookies."

Jeff stood at the kitchen entrance as Lauren and the rest of the women got up from the floor. Flour covered everyone and everything in the room, making for Captiva island's first white Christmas.

"I can see that."

The women remained frozen in place waiting for either Lauren or Jeff to say something.

"Hello, Lauren."

At that moment, Maggie stepped up and turned to the others.

"Why don't we all go outside and use the outdoor shower to get this stuff off?"

Everyone scuttled as fast as they could to the lanai. Before she left the room, Brea turned to Lauren.

"Listen for the kids upstairs will you, Lauren?"

Lauren nodded. "Of course."

The room was empty except for Lauren and Jeff. Lauren

waited for Jeff to speak, but when he did, she wasn't prepared for his question.

"Who is Callum Foster?"

Although she knew that she and Jeff would talk about Callum, Lauren wasn't ready to have their conversation under these circumstances. Covered from head to toe in white flour was not how she pictured herself when they finally saw each other again. She wanted quiet and privacy and a shower before they could each finally have their say.

And so, they put off their talk until everyone had cleaned up and Chelsea's house was put back the way it was before the food fight. Chelsea packed a bag for herself and Olivia and Lily. Everyone made their way back to Sebastian's, but Maggie stopped on her way out and placed her hand on Lauren's face.

She didn't say anything; instead, she smiled. Lauren placed her hand on top of Maggie's and knew in that moment that all was forgiven. She watched her mother and the others leave, and then turned to Jeff.

"Before I answer your question, why don't you explain to me who that woman was you were having lunch with?"

"What woman?"

"Don't play stupid with me, Jeff. I saw you. I was on my way to the office, and I had to drive through town. I saw you with a woman having lunch at Rory's Pub."

"You saw that?"

"I saw her push your hair from your face so don't tell me that this was someone you weren't intimately involved with. Who is she?"

"She's Kel Jenning's mother, Jackie. You know Kel, she's Olivia's friend from school. Her mother has been flirting with me for months. I told her that I'm a happily married man, but she wouldn't give up. She kept calling me and telling me that she's available to have an affair with and that no one needs to know."

Lauren couldn't believe what she was hearing. Although she'd suspected and worried herself sick over it, nothing could prepare her for his words.

"So you finally gave in?"

"What? No. I didn't give in. Of course not."

"Then what was all that in the restaurant?"

"She kept texting me and emailing me and trying to find opportunities for the two of us to be conveniently alone. You know how it is. Lots of school functions where we'd be thrown together over and over. Some of those weren't coincidences, I'm convinced. I started to get nervous around her. It felt like some unhealthy obsession, and I needed her to stop."

"And so, you thought going to a restaurant and letting her put her hands on you was a good idea?"

Jeff got up from his chair and walked toward her.

"I had a great idea. Remember when I tried to get you to free up your time so we could have lunch together? I thought I'd agree to meet with her but would bring you along and we'd confront her together. I kept trying to get you alone so I could explain what was going on and talk to you about my plan, but you kept canceling on me. I was desperate to get her to leave me alone. In the end I had to be rude and insulting which I hated but I think she finally got the message. That brings us back to my initial question. Who is Callum Foster?"

Lauren struggled with two truths. The first was determining how they got where they were. She knew she had a part in their marriage problems, but she couldn't see a clear or easy solution. The second was that she had to explain why Callum's attention made her feel special, and that too wasn't easy.

"Callum is, or I should say, was, a client of mine. He wanted to be more, and just like Jackie Jennings, he wouldn't stop pursuing me. I finally told him he'd need to find a different real estate agent because I wouldn't work with him any longer."

"So, maybe your experience will help you to understand mine."

Lauren knew that was an easy way out. It wasn't as simple as that.

"Not so fast."

"Huh?"

"Jeff, what I mean is that I'm willing to admit that I liked the attention I got from Callum. I'm sure that's true of anyone who's being pursued by a good-looking or attractive person. Unless you're also willing to accept that a small part of you enjoyed Jackie's advances, then I'm not sure we can move forward. Can't you be honest about that?"

Jeff took a minute to think about what she'd said.

"Ok, so it felt good getting all that attention, but that doesn't mean I would do anything about it. I happen to love my wife, and the life we've built."

Lauren had only one more question.

"Why didn't you return my calls? I was stubborn and angry, but after some time thinking about it, I wanted to talk with you and deal with whatever this was. You wouldn't talk to me. Why?"

"Well, the first time you called, I was angry too. Angry that you took the girls and left me during the holidays, and then when I worried you might be having an affair, I went to your office after searching the house for any receipts or evidence of you cheating. I couldn't find a thing until I saw all the messages from Callum that Nell had for you. Then, the guy actually shows up at your office while I'm there. I was beside myself. I didn't know what to do. In the end, I figured the only answer was for me to come down here and talk to you in person. This stuff isn't exactly the kind of thing you email or text."

Lauren sighed and sat at the counter. The stress of the last few days had caught up with her. So much of what her marriage had endured could have been avoided with compromise and communication. She struggled with how complicated and yet, simple, the origin of their troubles seemed to be, and wondered what they should do now. Jeff pleaded with her.

"All I know is that I want my family back. I don't know what the future holds, but I'm willing to do whatever it takes to work things out. How about you?"

"I want that too. I miss us."

Lauren wanted the comfort of his arms and the strength of his body against hers. For now, they would hold each other in a familiar embrace and promise to take every day one step at a time. It was the kind of promise they'd made so many years ago in front of family and friends and God. It was a promise to build a foundation that would see them into their later years. A foundation they hadn't broken, and from the looks of things was sturdier than either of them knew. She'd have to put her trust in that and have faith they'd find a way forward...together.

CHAPTER 24

The morning of Christmas Eve brought lots of excitement and chaos. Everyone staying at Sebastian's moved their things to the Key Lime Garden Inn. Chelsea cleaned up after the Wheeler clan had gone and locked the doors. When she was done, she made her way to the inn and stood in a breakfast buffet line with the others.

Maggie looked over the room to make sure everyone had what they needed. She found Chelsea at the end of the line and grabbed a plate for herself.

"You'll have to thank Sebastian again for me. Now that everyone is here, they're all going to wish they stayed at his place. It doesn't bother me at all, but the tight squeeze might be too much for Emily."

"I wouldn't worry too much about her. If she managed to get through the food fight yesterday, I think she'll be able to handle herself."

Maggie hadn't had a chance to explain to anyone about Emily's autism, and this wasn't the time to talk about it. She hoped that Chelsea was right. Maggie liked Emily and didn't want to see her struggle while Emily was under her roof. She'd already felt a responsibility for the young woman even though she was technically an adult. Given their unusual situation, Maggie felt good that she could feel motherly toward her. Emily had officially joined her family without any awkwardness.

The original dining room table had been too small for Maggie's large family. Paolo worked with a cabinet and furniture maker to build a larger one. Thirteen chairs and two highchairs fit perfect around the table with a smaller children's table that overlapped into the living room.

Maggie grabbed a stoop and stood on top.

"Hey, everyone. Look at me and smile. I need to capture this picture for my scrapbook. Say cheese!"

Everyone yelled cheese and then Maggie went into the living room to get a separate picture of the kids.

The clattering of forks against plates over multiple conversations made Maggie smile, but when she looked at Emily's face she could tell the noises were too much for her. Maggie leaned over and whispered to her.

"Emily, would you care to join me in the other room for a minute? I'd like to show you something."

Emily nodded, got up from the table and followed Maggie.

"This is my special room. I come here to be alone with my books and my journal. That chair by the window is really special. A good friend had this room before me and when she gave it to me I was very happy because I felt like she knew how much I'd love it."

Emily seemed confused. "She gave you a room?"

Maggie corrected her. "She gave me this house, so yes, I guess she gave me this room. Do you like it?"

Emily nodded. "Can I sit in your chair?"

Maggie smiled. "Of course."

Emily slowly sat and let the cushions envelop her. She laughed.

"It feels like the chair is hugging me."

Maggie nodded. "I know what you mean. That's how it feels to me too. Isn't it great?"

Emily sat quietly for a few minutes before speaking again. When she did, Maggie was surprised to hear what was on her mind.

"I don't remember very much about my father. He used to visit me a lot when I was about six years old. At least that's what my mother said. I still have the toys he brought me though, like Henry."

"Who's Henry?"

"Oh, that's my teddy bear. My father gave him to me a long time ago, so I've kept that toy to remind me of him."

Maggie felt awful that Emily had suffered growing up because Daniel secretly divided his time between two families. Emily should have had as much attention as his other children, but circumstances made that impossible.'

"Emily, would you like to see pictures of your father?"

Her face lit up. "Do you have pictures of him?"

"I have photo albums of all of my children growing up and of their father—your father."

There had been countless times since Daniel's death when Maggie had to put aside her regrets about her former husband for the good of others. The more she did that, the easier it got. By now, reminiscing about Daniel would bring joy to Emily and the rest of her family as well.

They went back to join the others and Emily went to the buffet to get some scrambled eggs and bacon. She seemed more relaxed and so Maggie decided to announce to the group that as soon as they finished their breakfast they should all gather in the front room to enjoy old family photos and a few videos that Maggie had made into DVDs.

When everyone chose where to sit, Emily sat on the floor and up close to the television screen. The next few hours they shared stories about their childhood. Everyone laughed and teasingly fought when there were disagreements about specific shared memories. Emily focused her attention on pictures of Daniel.

When he appeared on video, Maggie would pause it and wait for Emily to have a moment with her father. She sat mesmerized by the images, and through her, gave Maggie and the rest of the family a renewed sense of appreciation for the man. Even Chelsea found it in her heart to share pleasant memories of Daniel. If Maggie had any understanding of how magical the afternoon had been, Chelsea's graciousness was proof of it.

The Powell family Christmas tradition was to open one gift on Christmas Eve and wait until Christmas Day to open the rest. Since Becca planned to join Christopher's family in a few hours, Becca's father made an exception.

"I'm so glad you came back to Captiva for Christmas, honey. I would have been pretty sad not to see you. Don't let your brothers fool you either. They've missed you just as much as I have."

"Me too, Dad. I'm only sorry I wasn't here for the Christmas Festival parade. I understand Santa was a big hit this year."

Her brother Finn laughed at that.

"Yeah, Byron Jameson was seasick on the boat before we reached the kids on the beach."

Becca laughed. "No. You're not serious. A seasick Santa?"

Joshua joined in. "You should have seen it, Becca. He was throwing up on the way there. Dad had to grab Santa's beard and pull it off his head, so he didn't get it dirty. Can you imagine a Santa with vomit on his beard. The kids would have run away in horror."

Becca shook her head.

"I doubt it. There isn't much that will keep a kid away from getting his or her Christmas present from Santa Claus."

Her brother Luke jumped onto the sofa and peeled away the paper from his ice cream sandwich.

"What they forgot to tell you was that Byron had a few too many before the parade."

"Are you serious? How is it that no one noticed?"

"I don't think it was that no one noticed, I think it was too last minute to get another Santa, so they went with him. I heard that Marcus Werner wanted the job, but Byron did some negative campaigning against the guy. I've never seen such cutthroat behavior over playing Santa Claus. These people need to get a life. Anyway, I'm here now so go ahead, Becca, open your presents."

Finn handed her his gift first.

"This one's from me. I had to shop online to get it since I couldn't find any place that sold 'em down here."

"A matching purple hat, gloves and scarf set. I love it."

"Well, I know how cold it gets up in Massachusetts. I didn't know if you had these yet."

"You know me too well, Finn. I've been using my running shirt with the extended sleeves that you put your fingers through. I keep trying to find some time to shop but haven't gotten around to it. Thank you. It's perfect."

Joshua gave Becca his gift.

"I've been working on it for a while. I hope you like it."

Becca pulled out a small wooden box lined with purple felt inside.

"You can put your jewelry in it or anything else I guess."

"Joshua, I didn't know you knew how to do this. Where have you been hiding this talent? I love it so much, and yes, I'll probably put jewelry in it. Thank you."

Luke searched for his gift to give Becca but couldn't find it.

"I know I put it under the tree just last night. I don't understand."

Finn and Joshua tried to keep from laughing, and it soon became obvious to everyone that they'd hidden Luke's gift.

"Very funny, guys. Where is it?"

Finn pulled the thin rectangular box from under the sofa and handed it to Becca.

"Here you go, Becca. How awesome could this gift be if it can fit under the sofa?"

Luke knocked Finn over and jumped on top of him.

Becca laughed at the scuffle. "Nice to see nothing's changed around here."

Becca opened the box and moved the delicate tissue aside. She held up the soft lavender cashmere sweater for all to see.

"Luke, this is gorgeous."

She rubbed the fabric against her cheek.

"It's so soft."

Luke made a face at Joshua.

"I didn't buy it online either. I went all the way into the Miramar outlets to buy it for you. There's a gift receipt inside if you need to exchange it before you go back north."

"I love it. Thank you all so much."

She kissed her brothers and organized her gifts, closing boxes and trying to re-wrap what she could.

Crawford found his gift under the tree and handed it to Becca.

"I had this made for you, honey. I hope you like it."

Becca slowly unwrapped the box and opened it. A necklace with a single diamond surrounded by a gold dolphin was inside.

"I had your mother's engagement ring made into a necklace. I should have had this made years ago, but I held onto it because... well, I guess I didn't want to let go."

"Oh, Dad. It's perfect. Thank you so much."

She wrapped her arms around her father and gave in to the

sadness for just a moment. Before she got on the plane to return to Captiva, she'd promised herself there'd be no crying on this trip. Her father had made that impossible. Another holiday without her mother, grandmother and Gran reminded her to cherish life and all those who she loved most.

"Life is for the living," her Gran would say. Becca worked hard to live her best life in Boston, and she hoped with each passing Christmas the memories of the past would only strengthen the bonds within her family.

CHAPTER 25

*I*t wasn't necessary for everyone to get dressed up, but Maggie saw that her children decided it was appropriate to look as polished and formal as possible for Christmas Eve. Chelsea looked stunning in a sparkling jacket that accentuated her curves, something jackets rarely did.

"You look amazing, my dear. I hope you plan to send Sebastian a picture of you in this outfit."

Chelsea winked at Maggie.

"That, among others."

Shaking her head, Maggie walked away from Chelsea and looked for her husband.

She couldn't tell if someone was pulling a practical joke on Paolo or if he truly thought his sweater was the right choice for the evening. Pulling him aside, she whispered in his ear.

"Did someone tell you we were wearing ugly Christmas sweaters tonight?"

He shook his head. "Nope. I just thought it looked festive. Don't you like it?"

Not wanting to hurt his feelings she softened her approach.

"It's not bad. I just think with everyone dressing up for the evening, you'd like to wear something a little less...Ugly."

Paolo tried not to laugh but when Beth and Christopher joined in the fun, he couldn't contain himself. It was then that Maggie realized she was the target of their joke.

"Very funny, you guys."

Paolo pulled the sweater off over his head and displayed a crisp white shirt with tie.

Beth couldn't stop laughing.

"Mom, you should have seen your face when he walked into the room wearing that thing."

Riley and Grace had prepared a huge Christmas buffet, complete with beef tenderloin, pork with cranberry and roast turkey. There were Creole scallop cakes and bacon-wrapped blue cheese shrimp and curried mushroom empanadas for appetizers. There was so much food, Maggie assumed there would be several containers of leftovers which worked perfectly for her always-ravenous children the next day.

Jeff approached Maggie and they embraced. He seemed nervous as he whispered his thanks for taking care of Lauren, Olivia and Lily.

"I'm so sorry to have put you and Paolo through such worry. I know that Lauren and I are going to work things out. Nothing is more important than my family. I hope you know that."

"I know that Jeff. I've done my best to stay out of my children's business, but sometimes a girl needs her mother. That's why she came to me. It was probably less about her running away from something and more about running toward something. I'm glad that's how she explained it, anyway."

"It certainly is a better way to think about it. I'd never want my wife to think that she needed to run away from me. We've got some work to do on that. I want her to run to me when she's feeling that way. I get it, that I was the one who was doing the hurting, but we talked about it and I'm sure we've come to an understanding, at least I hope we have."

Maggie hugged Jeff once more and watched her family enjoy the food.

Riley and Grace came into the room.

"Merry Christmas, everyone."

Everyone returned the sentiment and Maggie walked them to the front door. She handed two envelopes to them.

"It's not much, just a little bonus to say thank you for everything you do around here. You both have helped me so much this year. I don't think the inn could have gotten off the ground without your delicious cooking. I hope you and your family have a wonderful Christmas."

They hugged and Maggie watched them get into a car and drive away. Until January 2nd, Maggie and her family were on their own in the kitchen. Riley and Grace had previously prepared several meals for her and Paolo and a few additional days' worth of meals for the rest of the family. With so many leftovers, Maggie didn't worry about running out of food.

After dessert and coffee, Maggie lit the fireplace in the living room and Emily surprised everyone by playing Christmas songs on the piano.

"Emily, I didn't know you played the piano."

"My mother insisted I learn to play. I can play several instruments actually. She must have thought I was going to start a musical band or something. Anyway, it turns out I have a talent for music, so I had lots of private lessons."

It was hard not to spontaneously burst into singing but it surprised Maggie to see Emily gather everyone into a more orchestrated performance. Even the children joined in. Christopher, always the prankster, asked, "Do you know *Santa Got run Over by a Reindeer?*"

Emily grimaced and shook her head.

"That's awful. I like Away in a Manger. It tells you what the holiday is about. I like that better."

Chelsea sat on the arm of Maggie's chair and placed her hand on her back.

"Well my friend, it looks like you got your Christmas wish. How does it feel?"

Maggie put her hand on Chelsea's arm.

"Isn't it wonderful, Chelsea? Looking around the room with everyone having fun and drinking eggnog, it almost looks like a Christmas card. Am I being sappy?"

Chelsea laughed and pulled the ottoman close so that she could sit on it.

"No, not sappy. You're a very lucky woman to have so many people who love you. There's nothing sappy about that."

Maggie struggled to keep from tearing up.

Whispering to Chelsea, she said, "I don't think I can do it, Chelsea. Everything is perfect. I can't ruin this night."

"Maggie you do what you want to but if you'll let your best friend give you unsolicited advice…"

"Chelsea, isn't most of your advice to me unsolicited?"

Chelsea shrugged. "You have a good point. What I mean is that if you look around this room, you can see your reason for everything that you do. Whatever that darn Code Red thing is, your children came to Captiva to be here for you. Oh, sure, I've no doubt they wanted to help Lauren too, but your kids aren't stupid. They knew you wanted them here, and they came. You're going to need all of us to get through the next few months. For once, please stop thinking of everyone else and focus on your needs."

Chelsea was right. She'd worked hard to gain her independence and to her that meant never letting her guard down. Being vulnerable felt uncomfortable but cancer had a way of knocking down the walls she'd built these last two years. It didn't mean she wouldn't fight, but it did mean that she'd need more in her army than just herself.

"I want to wait until the children have gone to bed. I'll tell them then."

Chelsea got up from her seat and smiled.

"Everything is going to be fine; you'll see."

The lump in Maggie's throat told her otherwise. The minute she was diagnosed with cancer, nothing was the same. She wasn't fine, and this Christmas was about to become a memory she never thought she'd have to make.

"You know what happens if you don't go to sleep? Santa Claus won't come and then no one will get any presents."

Michael wasn't the only one trying to convince the children it was time for bed. Brea followed his lead, and Sarah watched as Noah listened closely to her brother's warning.

"Is that true, Mommy?"

"Yup, Uncle Michael is right."

Even Olivia and Quinn chimed in. Being the oldest, they had previous Christmas Eve experience, and took the rules seriously.

"Come on, Noah. You have to go to sleep right away," Olivia said.

Cora and Lily did everything their big sisters said and wasted no time climbing the stairs to their bedrooms.

Trevor held Noah's hand as they followed behind Cora and Lily.

Maggie put her arm around Sarah's waist.

"Thank you for agreeing to stay here tonight. I can't wait to see Noah's face when he sees the gifts under the tree."

"I think Noah is getting the wrong impression. So far, Santa has made stops at Trevor's parents' place, our house and now the inn. I think he's going to look under complete stranger's Christmas trees in search of his gifts."

Two bowls of eggnog sat in the middle of the dining room table. One with brandy and the other without. Maggie chose the one with brandy and went back to her chair by the fireplace. It took a while for the children to be settled into their beds.

Becca came into the living room, and Christopher joined her.

"Hi, sweetie. How is your family?"

"They're great. Not much changes at the Powell home. I told them that you and I would come by tomorrow to celebrate with them. How are things here? Looks like there is plenty of food."

"Did you eat?"

"Of course. My father got Chinese food take-out. Typical for my family. Mind if I take a look at the buffet? I could use a bit of normal holiday food."

Christopher and Becca went into the dining room and slowly the rest of the family came downstairs.

Maggie waited until everyone was settled and enjoying the quiet. Emily stopped playing piano and joined her siblings on the sofa. Gabriel said he was hungry again and considered going back into the dining room, but Beth stopped him.

"There will be plenty of dessert in a bit. Just hang in there. You won't starve, I promise you."

Jeff sat next to Lauren, and she rested her head on his shoulder. Life was getting back to normal for her daughter and Maggie looked forward to hearing more good things from those two.

Paolo sat on the arm of Maggie's chair and put his arm around her shoulder.

Maggie's mother rubbed her stomach.

"I don't think I could eat dessert or anything else. I'm stuffed."

"Gabriel doesn't have that gene, Grandma. I don't think he knows what it's like to be stuffed. I don't know where he puts it all since he's so skinny."

With a serious expression, Gabriel said, "I have a fast metabolism."

Christopher followed Becca into the living room. She sat at the desk so that she had a place for her plate of food.

Chelsea stood near and smiled at Maggie. Maggie knew it was her way of saying, "it's time."

She got out of her chair and stood in front of the fireplace. Paolo stood beside her. She looked around the room and then cleared her throat.

"Guys, I'm so happy that we all got to be together this Christmas. I know I didn't handle things well. I'm sorry if I messed up anyone's Christmas. I guess I acted a bit selfish using the Code Red."

Lauren interrupted her.

"Although I have to admit that it warms my heart to think you all set out to do this for me. I really do appreciate it. I love you guys."

Christopher responded.

"Even Beth?"

Beth threw a chair pillow at him, and he caught it and threw it back. She looked at Maggie.

"Sorry, Mom. He's your son, so I blame you."

Maggie smiled and looked down at her hands, suddenly nervous about saying the words out loud.

"I didn't know it when I first called you all to ask you to come down to Captiva, but since that initial call, I, um…, I had a concern about something, so I went to the doctor. It seems that I have breast cancer."

The room went quiet.

Sarah spoke first.

"No. Mom. Are they sure?"

Maggie nodded.

Lauren was next.

"What did the doctor say?"

ANNIE CABOT

"He said that it's early. They caught it early, but I have to decide about the surgery. There are lots of details that I don't want to get into tonight, and Chelsea and I are going to see Carl's oncologist for a second opinion. He's making time for me on the 28th. I'll know more then."

Beth ran to Maggie and threw her arms around her.

"Mommy."

In the blink of an eye, her youngest daughter reverted back to her childhood. Beth hadn't called Maggie, Mommy in years.

The others came to her in rushed movements. One by one, holding her and sobbing. Emily was the only one who stayed back, uncertain of what to do. Maggie's mother waited until the others had stopped hovering. Her usual tough exterior and sarcastic retorts had been tucked away for another time. For now, the matriarch of the family held her daughter in a loving embrace.

"You're a Garrison. We're strong people—the women especially. You're going to beat this thing, you mark my words."

"Thanks, Mom."

The mood of the room was depressing and exactly what Maggie had wanted to avoid.

"Listen, everyone. This isn't a death sentence. I feel perfectly fine. The fact that they caught this early means I have an exceptional chance of getting it gone for good. I don't want you all crying over this. I didn't even want to tell you tonight. I thought it would spoil Christmas, so please, can we celebrate like we used to? I want to hear laughter in this house tonight or I'm going to return all your Christmas gifts. There will be nothing under the tree for any of you tomorrow morning. Got it?"

Her kids laughed and nodded their heads in agreement.

"My mom had breast cancer. I was twelve when she had it. She's all better now though. You're going to get better, Maggie," Emily said.

It was a simple and yet sincere response to Maggie's situation, and Emily's innocence warmed her heart.

"Thank you, Emily. I'm glad your mother is better, and you're right, I'm going to get better too."

"Hey, does everybody know what time it is? It's time for *Never Have I Ever*. I'm going first." Michael said.

Beth shook her head.

"Why do you get to go first?"

"Because I'm the oldest male."

"What?"

Maggie turned to Paolo and let the shouts and laughter fade in the background. They embraced and she nestled her face in his shoulder. Looking beyond to the other side of the room she saw Chelsea. Her best friend smiled and gave her a thumbs up.

CHAPTER 26

*W*ith so many kids in the house, the adults expected to be up before sunrise on Christmas Day, but that didn't happen. Instead, Maggie puttered in the kitchen preparing the batter for her cinnamon rolls with maple frosting. As if it were any other day, Chelsea appeared at the back door ready for her morning coffee.

"Merry Christmas, Chelsea. Come on in."

Chelsea kissed Maggie on the cheek and juggled several boxes in her arms. She peered through the door leading to the dining room and whispered,

"No one's up yet?"

Maggie shook her head.

"No, thank goodness. I'm not ready. I've got to put out a bunch of food that Riley and Grace left for us. Go put those gifts under the tree and come and help me with all this stuff."

Chelsea tiptoed to the tree and placed her boxes under the balsam fir. She stood back and took a picture with plans to send the photo to Sebastian later in the day.

She joined Maggie in the kitchen and got a coffee mug.

"I haven't had my first cup yet. You don't want me to do any work without it. So, how did things go after I left last night?"

"It was great. I started to yawn around 11:30 but everyone was still playing games. I'm not sure which one of my kids brought out the Twister game, but when Paolo and I went off to the carriage house, they were all on the floor."

"Even Christopher?"

"No. I'm sure he wanted to join in the fun, but he and Becca watched from the sofa. I don't know how many games we played last night, but when they got tired of one game they went into the den and pulled out something else."

Chelsea filled her coffee mug.

"I wish I had that kind of energy. Not sure about Twister though. At my age, once I'm on the floor you'd have to get a crane to get me up."

After a few sips of her coffee, Chelsea took a deep breath and put her arms out.

"Ok. What do you want me to do?"

"Here, take this lighter and light the Sterno cans under the trays. After that, take those pitchers of orange juice and cranberry juice and put them on the sideboard."

Just as Chelsea walked out of the kitchen, Maggie could hear stirrings in the living room. She pushed the door a crack and saw Sarah holding Sophia as Trevor cautioned Noah to wait for everyone else to come downstairs.

"Good morning, Noah. Well, will you look at the presents under the tree. Looks like Santa Claus has been here. Oh, look!"

A small table set up near the tree had a glass of milk and a plate of cookies. Santa had eaten most of the cookies with a bite out of the last cookie with crumbs the only thing remaining. The milk was gone but a small card with Santa's photo on the front and the words, "Thank you," on the back sat next to the glass.

Noah's eyes went wide with excitement.

"Daddy, can we wake up everybody now?"

Trevor was just about to answer when Olivia, Quinn, Cora and Lily came barreling down the stairs. Brea and Lauren in their bathrobes chased after them.

"Wait until everyone is here. You can't start without them."

Maggie watched as Sophia's eyes darted between one side of the room to the other. Too young to understand what all the excitement was about, she nonetheless looked ready to join her brother.

Sarah put her down and held her hand as she walked Sophia to the tree. Ever protective toward his sister, Noah bent down and talked to her.

"Santa Claus was here, Sophia. I bet there's a present under the tree for you. Mommy, can I help look for Sophia's present? I know how to spell her name. I can find it."

Noah dove under the tree in search of Sophia's present. He looked so proud of himself when he handed it to her.

With everyone present, the children grabbed their presents and soon wrapping paper was strewn around the room. Everyone had agreed ahead of time to forgo Christmas presents for the adults this year. Maggie announced that being together was gift enough. Instead, the only gifts under the tree were for the children.

Maggie watched her grandchildren playing with their toys and laughed when Trevor and Gabriel got down on the floor to play with the trucks and race cars.

Beth shook her head and looked at Maggie.

"I'm not sure who the real kids are, how about you?"

Brea let Jackson pull the wrapping paper off of his gift to find a big stuffed monkey inside.

"Wow, Jackson. Look at that."

She wiggled the toy on his nose and watched her son giggle. Looking at Maggie, she mouthed the words, "thank you."

Maggie nodded and clapped her hands, turning her attention to the group.

"I've got lots of delicious food in the dining room, so come join me whenever you're ready."

Paolo put the trays of scrambled eggs, sausages and roasted potatoes and pancakes on the sideboard.

Slowly, family members entered the dining room and filled their plates.

Maggie loved the chaos and hated to think in two days the inn would go back to its peaceful presence. She wanted to hold onto this moment forever, thus taking one photo after another.

Maggie had noticed during Emily's visit that she had excused herself from the group several times. She wondered if being with so many people all at once had been too much for her. She walked over to Emily to see if she needed anything.

"Have you been having a good time, Emily? I hope we haven't been too crazy."

Emily took a plate and got in line.

"I'm fine. My mother called me this morning to wish me a Merry Christmas. She said we'd open presents when I got back. She's coming home from Park City the day after tomorrow."

"That's lovely. I hope you'll have good memories of your visit here. I hope you come back again. Maybe just to relax and enjoy the beach. You all haven't had a chance to explore the island on this trip. Maybe next time?"

Emily nodded.

"I'll come back."

Maggie left her to enjoy her breakfast with the others and walked out of the room, looking for Paolo. He was cleaning up the living room and filling the trash barrel with wrapping paper and cutting up boxes for the recycle bin.

"I should have known you'd be in here tidying up. This can wait. Come and join us and have your breakfast."

They walked back into the dining room and got their food. Christopher and Becca got up from the table and walked over to Paolo and Maggie.

"Mom, we're going to take off for a bit. We promised Becca's family that we'd stop over for a visit. We're going to go over to the cemetery too."

"I want to visit my mother, Grandma and Gran. We're going to pick up some Christmas plants to leave at their graves."

"That's sound wonderful. Oh, wait. Chris, you got a letter the other day, let me get that for you."

Maggie ran to her desk and found the envelope addressed to Christopher Wheeler and family. She handed it to Christopher and watched as he opened the letter.

"It's a Christmas card from Nick Aiello's family. That's so sweet of them to think of me. I'll have to call them to wish them Merry Christmas."

"I think that would be great. I'm sure they'd love to hear from you. This is their first Christmas without their son. It has to be very hard for them."

Christopher nodded.

"I'm sure you're right. Anyway, we better get going. We'll be back later tonight."

Chris and Becca waved to everyone in the dining room.

"We'll see you all later. We're going over to Becca's family for a bit."

Before they walked out the door, Maggie stopped them.

"Becca, please tell your father and brothers Merry Christmas from us, will you?"

"Of course. Thank you, Maggie."

The last time Christopher saw Crawford Powell, he let him know that he loved Becca and was heading to Boston to be with her. Now, he returned to the island with the woman he loved by his side. It was incredible to Christopher that so much had changed in his life these last few months.

He had been training for the Boston Marathon outside but since the winter weather up north made that impossible he took his passion indoors at a local health club. Initially, he'd spent hours getting used to his prosthetic device and subsequently the blade that helped get him ready to run again. Those hours proved challenging at first, but now, he'd settled into a rhythm and routine that encouraged him to keep going.

Becca's support had meant everything to him, and he was convinced he'd never entertain the idea of running the marathon without her. His sister Beth had been a tremendous help as well, and their foundation on behalf of abused children was thriving. He loved volunteering at Summit Dreams and had met many wonderful people along his journey to wholeness.

Falling in love with Becca was the best thing that had ever happened to him, and although it had taken him a long time to get his head straight, he didn't take one moment with her for granted. He wanted to be with her for the rest of his life and was convinced that she felt the same.

Crawford Powell met them at the door. He hugged Becca and then Christopher.

"Hey, Christopher. Nice to see you again. I'm so glad you guys stopped by. We've still got lots of leftover Chinese Christmas food if you want some."

Becca laughed at her father.

"Dad. That's not a thing. There is no such thing as Chinese Christmas food. Besides, no one wants Chinese food on Christmas."

"What? Sure they do. Didn't you ever see that movie with the kid who wanted a BB gun? Don't they eat Chinese food at the end of that movie?"

"Well, yeah, but that's only because the dog ate their turkey and they had no choice."

Becca's brothers joined them and laughed at their father's idea of what holiday food looked like. They all settled into the living room. White Christmas was on the tv, and Luke was eating a plate of Chinese food.

"So, Mr. Powell, I was thinking about your classic car the other day. You have no idea how lucky you are to be living in Florida instead of the northeast. It's not that we don't have classic cars up there, but they've got to be covered and in a garage to survive the cold weather and snowstorms. Do you have to do much work to maintain it?"

Christopher worried that Becca might think it strange to bring up her father's classic car, but he needed a moment alone with the man and had no other way to get him outside.

"Would you like to see her?"

"Yeah. I didn't get much time to look it over when I was here before; I'd love to get a real good look at it."

"Well, come out back to the garage and let me show her to you."

Christopher looked at Becca.

"You don't mind, do you?"

Becca shrugged. "No, of course not, but since when are you interested in classic cars?"

As he got up to follow her father he smiled.

"Are you kidding? I love classic cars. I wish I had one myself."

When they reached the garage, Christopher wasted no time in getting right to the point.

"Mr. Powell…"

"Chris, call me Crawford, will you?"

"Uh, ok. Um, Crawford, I wanted to tell you…to ask you…if it would be all right with you if I asked Becca to marry me. So, um…would it?"

"Does Becca know that you came over here to ask me this?"

"What? No. Of course not. I'm not even sure exactly when I'm going to ask her, it's just I didn't want to do it without talking to you first. I want to do this right."

Christopher was starting to sweat. He didn't have much time

and worried that Becca might come out to the garage before they finished talking.

"Chris, I knew when you came to me before you left for Boston that you loved Becca and that one day we'd be having this conversation. You have my blessing. I'm sure Becca will say yes when you ask her. Just let us know when that happens because I want pictures and details. Understood?"

Christopher could breathe again.

"Thank you, Crawford. It means a lot to me that you approve, and I know how much it will mean to Becca."

"Welcome to the family, Chris."

They shook hands and then hugged. As they walked back into the room, Christopher took one more step toward the future he wanted more than anything. When the time was right, he'd propose to Becca, and to give his mother a Christmas gift that would make her happy, he'd share this private news with her before they headed back to Boston.

CHAPTER 27

*a*fter watching Olivia and Lily fall asleep in the middle of the living room floor, Lauren and Jeff carried them upstairs to bed. The hours of sugarplums dancing in their heads had long passed and now what was left were exhausted children and tired parents.

"Can you imagine we get to do this all over again when we get home?"

Since her mother's announcement the night before, Lauren couldn't get Maggie out of her mind. She felt helpless to do anything about the cancer, but it didn't keep her from searching for a way to help. Lauren formulated a plan in her mind and was nervous to run it by Jeff. They'd already gone through so much in the last few weeks, and she couldn't ignore that they needed time to work through their marriage troubles.

They tiptoed out of the girls' bedroom and Jeff pulled Lauren into an embrace. He kissed her and ran his hand up and down her back.

"I've missed you so much. I can't wait to get back home and find our new normal."

"Jeff, I need to talk to you about that."

She pulled away from him and walked across the hall and into their bedroom.

"I wonder if that new normal can wait a few more weeks."

"What?"

"I want to stay here with Mom for a while. Just long enough to get her through the surgery. She's going to need help with the inn, and Sarah's pregnancy and work at the Outreach Center, not to mention taking care of Noah and Sophia is too much."

He sighed and reached for her.

"Lauren, I understand your concern about Maggie, and I can appreciate how much you must be worried for her, but you've got a family back home that needs you. Part of our problems have been because we've been separated in our day-to-day lives. What happens if the distance creates a bigger crack in something that's already taken a pretty big hit?"

She pulled him to the edge of the bed and held his hand.

"Jeff, if I've learned anything about us after all this, it's that we're tough. Our marriage is stronger than we realized. But you're right, we've had a rough patch and I'm not trying to make light of it. That's why I want to suggest something. When I get back to Boston, I'm going to cut back on my working hours. The business is doing well, and there is no way I need to be away from you and the girls as much as I have."

"Really? Are you sure?"

"I'm positive. I want more time with you than the occasional date night."

He shrugged and smiled at Lauren.

"I guess we can get along without you for another few weeks but promise me we'll video lots until you get home."

"Thank you, Jeff. I mean it. This means a lot to me."

Her ran his finger down her cheek and kissed her lips.

"Anything for the love of my life."

❄

Maggie did everything she could in the last few hours with her family to keep all discussions upbeat and cheerful. Inside, her heart was breaking, and she'd felt like crying several times during the night.

In the back of her mind she'd always known there would be times when the distance between her and her children would prove problematic. It was inevitable that she would encounter challenges she'd need to face on her own, but a cancer diagnosis never entered her mind.

Her emotions were all over the place, and the last thing she considered was how she'd be able to handle the business of running the inn. She hadn't shared her health issues with Riley and Grace but that would have to change...and soon.

As Maggie stood in front of the Christmas tree, Lauren and Jeff stood beside her. Lauren put her arms around her mother's waist and squeezed her tight.

"Mom, Jeff and I have something we'd like to talk to you about."

Maggie turned to look at the two of them.

"Is everything all right?"

"Yes, everything is fine. Jeff is going to take the girls back to Boston, and I'm going to stay here for a few weeks."

"What? Why? I thought the two of you worked things out."

"We did. We're great. It's just that I want to stay here with you for a few weeks. Just long enough to get you through the surgery. You're going to need help running the inn, and with Chelsea leaving for Paris and Sarah so busy with her work and family, it makes sense that I stay on for a little while."

Maggie couldn't believe what she was hearing. She'd never ask any of her children to sacrifice their lives for her, but here her daughter was, putting her mother's needs before her own.

"I...I don't know what to say."

Lauren hugged Maggie.

"You don't have to say anything. Jeff and I are happy to do this for you. I can't thank you enough for everything you've done for me all my life. You've been right by my side every step of the way. I'm so proud that you're my mother. It's time I show you just what you mean to me."

Maggie didn't bother fussing about the tears that fell on her face. Overcome with emotion, she'd finally come to terms with the roller coaster that had become her life. Some days were harder than others, but she didn't want to miss one minute of what life threw her way.

Laughing, she looked around the room.

"I need a tissue."

Lauren ran to get a box for her mother. While she was gone, Maggie took the opportunity to say something to Jeff.

"I never believed for one minute that you cheated on Lauren. I'm not sure if you care, but I thought you should know."

Jeff smiled at his mother-in-law and nodded.

There wasn't much more to say than that.

After dinner, Emily searched for Maggie.

"I just wanted to thank you for making me feel so welcome in your home. I'm not dumb. I know how difficult it must have been when you first heard about me."

Maggie had often thought about the day of Daniel's funeral and how unbeknownst to her, Emily—a perfect stranger in Maggie's eyes— stood by her father's coffin.

"Emily, I remember seeing you at the cemetery. I didn't know who you were, but I could see on your face how sad his death was for you. I'm sorry you didn't feel able to approach the rest of us. Even though we didn't know you then, we were your family. I'm sorry that circumstances and Daniel's choices made that impossible."

"It's ok. I think we all moved on from that day."

Maggie had a thought.

"Wait. Emily, stay here and I'll be right back. I have something for you."

Maggie went to her jewelry box and searched for a bracelet. It had several charms on it and a large letter "W" for the Wheeler last name. She returned to Emily and gave her the bracelet.

"Your father gave this to me when I was about your age."

Emily looked confused.

"But it's yours. He gave it to you."

"Yes, but that was a long time ago when I became a Wheeler. You're a Wheeler too and you should have something from him. I know he'd be very happy to see you wearing it."

Emily threw her arms around Maggie. It was the first time during her visit that she let herself get this close to her.

Maggie helped put the bracelet on Emily's wrist.

"Thank you, Maggie."

"You're very welcome, Emily."

By the time everyone finished dinner, the girls had Rudolph the Red-Nosed Reindeer on tv. The men relaxed in the living room while the women went into the kitchen to clean up.

"Why do the guys get to sit down and do nothing while the women have to do all the work before, during and after we eat?" Beth asked.

"Because that's the way it's been done throughout history," Sarah responded.

Grandma Sarah reminded Maggie of a time when she was a teenager when her family tried to change that dynamic.

"Do you remember when your sister and you protested that very thing? Your father and brother said that us women were making a big deal about nothing, so they came into the kitchen and took the dishtowels from us and started drying the plates and putting them away. Your father rolled up his sleeves and started washing the dishes."

"Mom, I remember that a little differently than you do. I remember you and Aunt Louise getting very upset about that, taking the towels back and running the men out of the kitchen. I tried to stop Aunt Louise, but she insisted it was 'women's work,' I think she was worried about job security."

"Well our generation taught us that was our place. Today, if the men came in here to clean the kitchen, you wouldn't stop them."

Michael overheard the women and yelled to them from the living room.

"Yeah, well, we don't expect you to go outside and chop wood."

Brea put her hands on her hips.

"Really, Michael? When was the last time you chopped wood?"

Michael mumbled something to the effect of 'just saying' before he turned his attention back to Rudolph.

Christopher came into the kitchen and Beth pounced on him.

"Are you here to dry dishes? Here, take my towel."

"No thanks. Mom, can I talk to you for a minute?"

Maggie wiped her hands on her apron and followed Christopher into the den.

"Mom, I just wanted to let you know that when Becca and I went over to visit with her family, I asked Mr. Powell if he'd give me his blessing for me to ask Becca to marry me."

Maggie put her hand over her mouth to keep from screaming.

"Oh, Chris, this is wonderful. I'm so happy for you two. We all love Becca. When are you going to ask her?"

"I'm not sure just yet. I haven't even shopped for a ring. I just wanted to get his blessing now because I'm not sure when we'll be back down here. He was great and seemed happy about the whole thing."

"Don't tell me you were nervous?"

"Of course I was. It's not every day you ask your girlfriend's father if you can marry his daughter."

Maggie hugged her son and patted him on the back.

"Becca is a lovely young woman, but you're my son. She's getting a great guy."

"Thanks, Mom. Don't say anything to the others yet. I want to wait until I actually propose. Let's hope she doesn't say no."

Maggie rolled her eyes.

"Not likely."

She hugged him again and didn't want to let go. So many amazing things happened this Christmas. She felt like this was just another beautiful memory they'd made.

CHAPTER 28

The chaos and noise that started the minute Maggie's family arrived, now heralded the mass exit of the Wheeler clan. From the moment they descended upon the Key Lime Garden Inn, Maggie dreaded this day, and now here it was making her heart ache.

Lauren kissed Olivia, Lily and Jeff.

"Don't forget to video with me as soon as you get home." Chelsea added her two cents.

"That monitor is always up and ready for our lunch-bunch monthly meetings. It's yours now for as long as you need it."

Beth and Gabriel along with Michael, Brea, Quinn and Cora hugged her and then Paolo. Maggie rubbed Jackson's cheeks and kissed his nose.

"You promise to update us the minute you get more information from the new doctor, ok?" Beth insisted.

"I promise. Don't worry."

Christopher gave his mother a hug and a kiss and Becca hugged Maggie and then Lauren before walking toward the car.

Sarah and her family said their goodbyes and headed off-island. The rest of the family gathered their luggage and Paolo helped them into the vans.

As they were ready to pull out onto the street, Emily stuck her arm out the back window and wiggled her bracelet.

Paolo stood behind Maggie and wrapped his arms around her as they waved at the vans until they were out of sight. Maggie tapped Paolo's arm and leaned back against him. She blinked a few times to keep the tears from falling.

Chelsea put her arm around Lauren.

"How about you and I go back to my house so I can show you how things work and give you a set of keys?"

Lauren nodded and looked at Maggie.

"Do you need me to do anything, Mom?"

"No. I'm fine. I'm expecting Riley and Grace back this afternoon and need to get my hands dirty in the garden for a bit. You two go on, and I'll catch up with you later."

The ocean and her plants were her two sanctuaries, and so, Maggie walked to the carriage house and picked up her garden basket, hat and gloves and went into the garden. She knew before the day was over she'd visit both places and renew her sense of balance and calm. This time she'd go alone, and Paolo knew to leave her be when she was like this. Grateful for his love and support, she'd need Paolo more than ever in the coming months, but for now, she'd treasure this time alone with her journal and nature.

Looking through the refrigerator, Lauren made a list of food items to buy.

"I feel bad. My family and I have basically eaten all of your food. I'm making a list and then going to Jerry's in Sanibel. Is there anything you want me to get specifically?"

Chelsea didn't respond and so Lauren repeated her question.

"Do you want me to pick up something for you at Jerry's?"

Still no response.

Lauren closed the refrigerator and walked out of the kitchen and into the living room. Chelsea was sitting on the sofa, staring at nothing in particular.

"Chelsea? Are you all right?"

"What? Oh, I'm sorry, Lauren. Did you say something?"

"Um, yes I've said several somethings. I'm making a list so I can go to Jerry's and fill the refrigerator. I asked you if there was something in particular that you'd like me to get."

Chelsea turned and looked at Lauren.

"Do you think my going to Paris is a mistake? I mean, your mother would never ask me to stay, but do you think she'd want me to put it off and be here during her surgery?"

Lauren sat next to Chelsea and put her hand on her arm.

"No. I don't. I know my mother. She'd be pretty angry at you for putting this off. I know how you feel, Chelsea. You're her best friend and you love her. She loves you too, and because of that she wants what's best for you."

"I feel awful. I'm not sure I can enjoy this trip under these circumstances."

"Then fake it till you make it."

"What?"

"Pretend to be excited about this trip and once you're in Paris with the man that you love, you'll be happy you decided to go. Besides, mom told me that you don't have any particular time frame for when you return. I promise that I'll contact you myself if I think you should come home. Until then, go and enjoy yourself. Mom has me, Ciara, Sarah and Paolo. She'll be fine."

Chelsea nodded.

"I'm sure you're right. I just can't believe the awful timing on all this. I never would have even entertained the idea of going to Paris had I known about your mother. I didn't need to tell her about Sebastian's request and proposal."

"Sebastian proposed to you?"

Chelsea nodded. "He did. I said no, of course."

"Why, of course? You love him, don't you?"

"I do, very much, but I've had the love of my life. If you're lucky, you get one of those. When you do, that's pretty much it forever. As much as I love Sebastian, I don't want to be anything other than Chelsea Marsden, Carl's wife."

"I see you still wear your wedding ring. Doesn't that bother Sebastian?"

Chelsea shrugged.

"He never said, and I've never asked him. It better not though, because I'm never taking it off. I think you and Jeff have that kind of love. It's a solid foundation to having a life-long marriage."

Lauren smiled at that.

"I feel the same way. We just got through a horrific situation and yet, we're still going strong. Don't get me wrong, I know that we have some work to do, but I believe we'll get there. Anyway, what's the plan? When do you leave for Paris?"

Chelsea put her hands to her face.

"You know what? I have no idea. I've put off getting my plane ticket until we have more information from the doctor. Maybe the second opinion will tell her that she doesn't need surgery. That would be ideal."

Chelsea knew it was a long-shot, and she also knew that she was trying to convince herself that Maggie would be fine. No matter what the doctor said tomorrow, Chelsea would hold off on buying her plane ticket until she knew exactly what her friend was up against.

Two additional scans and several hours of waiting for results kept Paolo and Maggie on edge. She'd already had more coffee than usual, and cafeteria food did little to help her already frayed nerves. She'd answered a number of texts from her children, and finally had to ask Michael to be the point person for information. She promised everyone that when she got anything to report, she'd tell Michael and he could share the news.

A nurse came into the waiting area.

"Mrs. Moretti?

"Yes."

"Can you follow me, please?"

Maggie and Paolo followed her to a larger office just outside the exam room. They sat in the two chairs directly in front of the large desk and waited.

Maggie took deep breaths and closed her eyes. Suddenly upset with herself for not saying yes to the meditation classes Chelsea wanted to try, she did her own version of relaxation exercises.

The doctor came in and shook Paolo's hand and then Maggie's.

"Well, I can tell you that I concur with the first diagnosis. The cancer hasn't spread. This is the best-case scenario, however, the tumor is rather large making my recommendation that you have surgery to remove the breast. I've seen a lot of women with breast cancer, Mrs. Moretti and if it helps to hear this, I wish they all were caught this early. Have you any leaning one way or the other about what you want to do?"

Maggie wasn't prepared to decide on this today, but rather needed a second opinion on the diagnosis and prognosis.

"Is lumpectomy out of the question?"

"I know your doctor recommended that as a possible course of action, but I'd take that off the table. The tumor is much larger than we like to see. I know it's a difficult decision, but it is my opinion that mastectomy should be the next step."

From the moment her family doctor talked to her about her situation, she knew he was leaning in the direction of mastectomy. Maggie had hoped there was a chance for a lumpectomy, but hearing this new information confirmed what she believed to be her only choice.

"Thank you, doctor."

"You're very welcome, Mrs. Moretti. Let me know if I can help you further, and please give my best wishes to Mrs. Marsden. I remember her husband Carl. He was a good man."

Maggie nodded.

Without speaking, they left the doctor's office and made their way back to the car in complete silence.

Before he started the car, Maggie turned to face Paolo.

"Seems like the next step is calling my doctor to schedule the surgery."

"You've got your cell phone. Why don't we do that now?"

Maggie pulled her phone out of her handbag, noticing her shaking hands. She'd already made her decision before walking out of the building, but now, she sat frozen, unable to dial the phone.

Paolo took the phone from her and placed it on his lap. She looked into his eyes and saw so much love, she couldn't speak. She tried to talk but nothing would come out. Instead, for the first time since the diagnosis, she grabbed his shirt, fell into his arms, and sobbed like a baby.

CHAPTER 29

The day-to-day life at the Key Lime Garden Inn fell into its routine of preparing and organizing for new guests. As soon as she scheduled her surgery, Maggie focused on projects around the inn to keep busy. New Year's Eve was a quiet celebration between Paolo, Chelsea, Ciara and Lauren. Anxious to begin the next chapter of her life, Maggie made lists of things that needed doing during January and February.

Lauren's decision to stay on for a few weeks gave Maggie the chance to sit back and relax. Lauren joined Paolo in the garden and learned about the vegetables and flowers. Although Paolo handled most of that aspect of the property, Maggie felt it was important that Lauren understand how things worked in their garden-to-table preparations. Riley and Grace walked Lauren through their daily responsibilities and Sarah explained how the inn's computer software worked along with its basic bookkeeping and paperwork filing cabinet.

Chelsea stopped by several times during the week after New Year's and would soon leave for Paris. Maggie was happy for her friend, but already missed her even though she hadn't left yet.

With her surgery at the end of the week, Maggie, determined to get Chelsea on the plane before she changed her mind, kept pushing her friend to get packing, and to contact Sebastian about her imminent arrival. Whatever she needed to do to ensure Chelsea stuck to her plan, she was willing to do.

Ciara had been fairly quiet during Christmas and Maggie felt a tension between her sister-in-law and Paolo. Paolo and Ciara were as close as any brother and sister could be. They rarely disagreed on anything and as far as Maggie could tell, there had been no arguments of any kind. She decided to talk to Paolo about his sister as soon as he got back from Sanibellia.

For now, she let her body sink into the soft cushions of the outdoor loveseat and ignored the desire to ponder anything of significance. A soft breeze drifted through the porch, rustling the hanging plants as if to caress their colorful leaves. Across the yard a wall of trees separated her property from the next. Their branches moved in what looked like a dance on the lawn. She felt peaceful and wanted to hold onto the quiet for as long as she could, dreading the days to come that would challenge and possibly rob her sense of calm and contentment.

Being hovered over had already annoyed Maggie, and so she reminded herself it was because everyone loved and cared about her. She knew that the well-intentioned supervision had only just begun. She'd need to think of a polite way to convalesce without so many people constantly doing things for her.

Why is it so difficult to ask for help? You're not superwoman you know.

Paolo arrived and got out of his truck, running up the stairs to the porch and sat next to Maggie.

"You look comfortable."

"I haven't enjoyed this much relaxation in months. I think I could get used to this. How are things at Sanibellia?"

Paolo shrugged.

"The same. I got lots of works done so that's something."

Maggie sat up straight and massaged his shoulders.

"You seem tense. Is everything all right?"

"Yup. Just lots to do at work and around here. I'm trying to juggle it all the best that I can."

Undeterred, Maggie pushed further.

"Is everything ok between you and Ciara?"

Paolo hesitated before answering, and Maggie could feel his body tense.

"Yeah. Everything's fine. Why do you ask?"

"Because at Christmas the two of you seemed to avoid making eye contact or talking to each other. What's going on?"

She could tell he didn't want to talk about it, but she also knew that if he didn't, in time there'd be an unprovoked explosion.

"We had an argument after Thanksgiving but with everything that's gone on around here, I didn't want to talk about it. Even almost getting killed when that guy pulled a gun on her and Sarah wasn't enough for us to put our differences to rest."

"That's not like you and Ciara. What in the world could have made the two of you so upset with each other?"

Paolo turned to face her.

"Do you remember when we were in Italy, the guy that came over with his father to attend the funeral? Maurizio Bianchi?"

"Wasn't he the one I said was very handsome and looked like a movie star?"

"Yes. That's the one. I was surprised when he and his father came because, well, it's a long story but my family and their family have been enemies forever. My whole life, all I ever heard was what a terrible man Gustavo Bianchi was. His father before him hated Gustavo's father Antonio for some reason that we didn't know. When Gustavo had children, then my father would complain about them as well. When I asked my father what had happened to make our family loathe the Bianchi family so much, my father would only push me away and tell me to never bother him with such questions again."

"Let me understand this. Your family has been enemies with the Bianchi family for probably decades, but you don't know why?"

"No. I finally found out. It seems that it started with my grandfather. There was some bad blood about a woman that my grandfather was in love with. That woman married Antonio Bianchi, Gustavo's father. Maurizio's grandfather. From that moment on, anything that happened in Gaeta having to do with the Bianchis, my family would get angry over it. This has gone on to such an extent, that when Gustavo and Maurizio came to the funeral, everyone in my family was shocked. Apparently Gustavo has been in love with my mother since they were children. My father knew about it so you can imagine that here we are again with another problem between the two families."

Maggie tried to stay focused on the Moretti/Bianchi dispute, but scenes from The Godfather movie kept popping into her head.

"What exactly does this have to do with Ciara?"

"After my mother died, it seems that Maurizio has been communicating with Ciara on the computer. They've been talking for months now behind my back. And now, he wants to come to America, to Captiva, to see Ciara. She says she's in love."

"Behind your back? My goodness, Paolo, Ciara is a grown woman. She doesn't need your permission to speak to Maurizio, who is clearly a nice young man to come to your mother's funeral under such circumstances. I think it would be wonderful for him to come here. Ciara has always been so busy working and caring for others. I think it's wonderful that she has romance in her life."

Paolo's face turned several shades of red, and it was the first time Maggie had ever seen her husband angry about anything. Instead of talking to her about it, he tried to control his temper, and took a few deep breaths before excusing himself to work in the garden. The conversation was over whether Maggie wanted it to be or not.

Lauren came outside to join her mother and sat on the porch swing.

"I thought I heard you and Paolo talking. Where is he?"

Maggie pointed to the tomato plants.

"He's out there working in the garden. I wouldn't talk to him right now. He's working out his problems."

Lauren leaned forward and squinted.

"He is? He looks more like he's talking to the tomato plants."

Maggie nodded.

"Yup. That's what I said."

Maggie didn't care how much time it took to get off the island. A drive to the Outreach Center had become necessary after her conversation with Paolo. She dialed Sarah's number and was glad she'd caught her before lunch.

"Hey, Mom. Is everything ok?"

"Yes, I'm fine. I wondered if Ciara and you would like to go to lunch with me today?"

"Oh, wow. Yeah. That would be great. Are you sure you feel up to driving all the way to the Center? We could come to you if you'd rather."

Maggie knew having Ciara anywhere near her brother right now was a mistake.

"Nope. I'm looking forward to seeing you at your office. I haven't been there in a while. How about we have lunch at that little pizza place near your building?"

"Sure. What time?"

"I'm already on my way. I should be to you in about twenty minutes."

"Ok. I'll let Ciara know. See you then."

Maggie ended the call and rubbed her shoulders. Anyone would tell her to mind her own business and to let Ciara and Paolo work things out on their own, but Maggie knew how important it was to have support on things that were important, and nothing was more important than helping her family in times of trouble.

As soon as Maggie arrived, Sarah and Ciara met her at the front door.

"Do you want to come in, or should we go to the restaurant now and I'll give you a tour after we eat?"

"Let's eat."

Sarah laughed. "I'm so glad you said that. I'm starving, but then again, these days, I'm always starving."

They were the first to enter the restaurant and found a table in the back corner of the room. They decided to share a large pizza as three tall glasses of water were placed in front of them.

"So, Mom. This is really something. I don't think you've ever driven into town."

"Well, I wouldn't go that far. I've driven into Fort Myers by myself before. I wanted to see my two favorite people, that's all."

Sarah shook her head. "Nope. That's not it. You didn't drive all the way here just to say hello. So, come on. What is it? And don't hem and haw either. You're scaring me."

"Sarah, this has nothing to do with me or with you."

The two women turned and looked at Ciara.

"Me? This has something to do with me? What have I done? I pretty much mind my own business, and…"

Ciara stopped mid-sentence. Maggie could see that Ciara understood exactly why she had come to talk with her.

"Maggie, I don't know what my brother has told you, but I don't think there's any chance of you changing his mind."

Sarah looked from one woman to the other.

"Ok, you guys. Someone better tell me what's going on."

Ciara looked at Sarah and sighed.

"I should have told you about this sooner."

Ciara explained everything to Sarah, while Maggie waited to share her earlier conversation with Paolo.

Sarah was shocked. "Oh, for heaven's sake. What century is this? Don't you think Paolo is making too much of this?"

Ciara nodded.

"He certainly is, but you don't know my brother. For as easy-going as he appears, he's still got a lot of our father in him. Trust me, our father isn't easy-going."

Maggie took Ciara's hand in hers.

"Ciara, what do you want? You are an adult and have every right to live the life you want, not the one Paolo wants. You know how much he loves you. I'm certain all of his concerns stem from his desire for you to be happy. The rest of this can be worked out. The first step is for you to decide what you want, and we'll help you make that happen."

Ciara had tears in her eyes.

"I want Maurizio to come to America. I want to be with him."

Maggie slammed her hand down on the table.

"Ok. Then that's what we'll help you with. You talk to Maurizio and figure out when he can come, and then let me know. Keep me in the loop—Sarah too—and we'll figure this out. One thing is for certain, your brother won't be able to deny you what you want when I'm done talking to him. Don't you worry about a thing. Before long, you and Maurizio will be together, and it will be your brother who will not only agree, but insist that he come to America."

Sarah and Ciara looked at Maggie as if she had two heads. Ciara shook her head.

"What? How in the world…?"

"Leave your brother to me. Now, let's eat pizza and enjoy our lunch."

It was hard to argue with her when she had a plan. Knowing

that she had surgery in a few days, and that her husband would do anything to help her through what was to come, she recognized leverage when she saw it. Was it beneath her to use her situation to manipulate Paolo? Probably. But she didn't let that stop her one bit.

CHAPTER 30

*M*aggie walked to Chelsea's house with a heavy heart. It would take everything she could muster to stay positive and upbeat about her friend leaving for Paris. This was no time to be selfish, and so she lifted her head and smiled. She waved to friends and business owners along the way. Christmas decorations still hung along Andy Rosse Lane.

Powell Water Sports was open, and she could see Crawford Powell explaining how to use a Jet Ski to a customer. He waved when he saw her, and she waved back.

When she got to Chelsea's house, Chelsea's luggage was already at the front door. Insisting they say their goodbyes here rather than at the airport, her friend had made a small brunch just for the two of them.

"Knock, Knock."

"I'm out here on the lanai."

Lifting a basket of scones, Maggie said, "I brought something to add to the table. You can take a few with you to eat on the plane and leave a few for Lauren."

She kissed Maggie's cheek. "I have to admit that your scones were on the top of my list of things I'm going to miss. By the way,

Byron Jameson came to say goodbye to me early this morning. He wanted to know if I'd be back before Easter because he was already planning an Easter parade."

"What, does he want to be the Easter Bunny now?"

"Don't make fun. I wouldn't put it past him."

"Well if he does, he'd better be sober. It's one thing to be a drunk Santa Claus, but I don't think anyone can stomach a drunk Easter Bunny."

Maggie looked over at where Chelsea's paintings usually sat.

"What did you do with your paintings?"

"I've got them put away upstairs."

It suddenly occurred to Maggie that Chelsea might not get time to paint while she was in Paris.

"How will you spend your time if you're not painting?'

Chelsea thought about it for a minute.

"Well, after we've exhausted all the tourist spots, he wants to take me to the country where his mother was born. Don't worry about me, I couldn't be in a better place if I want to paint. You can hardly walk in the city without running into an artist painting the Eiffel Tower or some Parisian landscape. It's the one thing I'm most excited about to be truthful."

"You mean seeing Sebastian isn't exciting enough?"

Chelsea smiled and didn't elaborate, instead her response was underwhelming.

"That will be nice too."

They sat at the table and Chelsea served Maggie a slice of quiche and then filled her bowl with fresh fruit. Even though neither of them had an appetite, Maggie knew her friend was trying her best to put on a happy face.

"I've made a pot of tea for us. I figured this wouldn't be a proper goodbye without your cup of tea."

Maggie watched her friend hold back tears, grabbed her arm and made her sit.

"Chelsea, stop. Please."

"Oh, Maggie, this isn't the way I wanted to go to Paris. I can't leave you, not now."

"Listen to me. Don't you realize that wherever you and I go in the world, we are never far from each other? You know, a while back I thought of you when I read something about friendship. I'm paraphrasing here, but it was something like this. Some people are meant to come into your life for a season. Just like the changing of the leaves on trees, they come and make an impact on your life, but then they go. There's nothing wrong with that. Others are like the trunk of the tree. They're sturdy, they hold the tree up with their strength and constant support. Year after year, they never waver. Dependable and true, they are always there. You were never meant to come into my life for just a season, Chelsea."

Chelsea's brow furrowed.

"What are you saying, that I'm a tree trunk?"

They both laughed at her question.

"Well, yeah. You're my tree trunk and I'm yours."

"Whew. That's a relief. I thought you were saying that I'm fat."

They both knew that Chelsea was doing what she needed to do to deal with the sadness between them. Laughter had always worked before, and this time they needed to laugh more than ever.

Maggie pointed out something else.

"There's nothing wrong with the people who come into our lives for just a season, Chelsea. They have their purpose too. The problem comes when we have expectations of those people to be our tree trunk when that's not the role they play."

"Maggie, do you think Sebastian was only meant to come into my life for a season?"

"I don't know. You're the only one who can answer that. Give it time. Maybe you'll know more after being in Paris with him."

Chelsea nodded. "I guess you're right."

A ring of the doorbell interrupted their conversation.

"That would be my airport driver."

The women got up from the table and hugged.

"Stay and enjoy the food, Maggie. Call Lauren over and ask her to join you. This house is hers for the next few weeks anyway."

Chelsea opened the front door, and let the driver take her luggage to the car. She turned and ran back to Maggie, and they hugged one last time.

"You promise to have either Paolo or Lauren call me the minute you get out of surgery; do you hear me? I'm going to need to know everything that's going on with you."

"I promise."

Chelsea took her handbag and walked to the front door. She turned one last time and smiled.

"You're more than my tree trunk, Maggie. You're my sister and my best friend and I love you."

And, with that, Chelsea walked out of the house, closing the door behind her.

Maggie didn't call Lauren. Instead, she cleaned Chelsea's kitchen and washed her barely used dishes. She didn't have an appetite and so she packaged up the food and put everything into the refrigerator. As soon as she was done, she went outside and sent Lauren a text letting her know that she'd need to come lock up the house. Maggie headed for the beach and the warmth of the sun. She stared out across the water and could see the Powell boys driving their boat and giving the tourists another para-sailing adventure.

The beach was crowded. The wind had died down and the ocean's delicate waves made getting into the water much easier. She smiled at the children playing in the sand and remembered back to when her children's fascination with the seashells and sand mirrored her love of everything to do with the sea.

Today, Maggie didn't feel like swimming. Instead, what she wanted were more moments like she had earlier in the day. The quiet calm of the porch swing and since the air was cool, a fuzzy blanket to wrap around her body.

When she reached the Key Lime Garden Inn, she went inside to see if Riley and Grace needed her for anything. Two new guests would check in at two o'clock, so she had time to relax and enjoy what remained of the morning.

"Hey Mom, I'm headed over to Chelsea's to lock up and then I'll be back. Why don't I check the guests in when they arrive? I might as well dive right in and start helping around here."

"I think that's a great idea, Lauren. In that case, I think I'll sit right here and enjoy the quiet."

"Sounds good. I've just asked Riley to make a pot of tea for you. She'll bring it out when it's ready. You just relax and do nothing for a change. Oh, and Paolo told me to tell you that he'll be back for dinner. He said he had some problem at Sanibellia that he had to deal with."

"Thanks, Honey. That's sweet of you. I think a cup of tea is exactly what I need right now."

Maggie didn't bother to mention that Chelsea had already offered tea less than an hour ago. She wasn't ready for it then, but now it was the perfect remedy for her sadness.

Change had never come easy to Maggie, and it seemed that didn't matter at all to the forces of nature. Whether she was ready or not, change was coming, and there was very little she could do about it.

Christmas had come and gone, and she felt proud that her family once again had come together to share their love and support for each other. There was so much to be grateful for, the least of which was the realization that she never had to invoke the Code Red at all.

All she had to do was call her children and tell them that she had cancer and needed them to be with her for Christmas this year. She had no doubt they would have dropped everything to be by her side, and that was not only the truest meaning of Christmas but was everything to her.

She pushed her heel down against the floor and gave the swing a good push. Rocking back and forth, she let the rhythm of the chair soothe her anxiety. Several weeks earlier she sat on this swing in the middle of the night.

Unable to sleep, she'd worried that something big was going to happen. She didn't know what it was that made her feel so uneasy. Now, with a new year beginning, she welcomed what she couldn't control with open arms. There was nothing left to do but breathe.

THE END

For a sneak peek at the next book in this series, check out the Prologue for Captiva Nights on the next page.

CAPTIVA NIGHTS

PROLOGUE

*C*iara Moretti never thought of herself as a romantic person. Her family had been her focus all of her life and there was nothing romantic about cooking and cleaning.

It wasn't that she didn't notice boys when she was a young girl living in Gaeta, Italy. It was that she had been forbidden to acknowledge their existence.

Her parents had been strict with her while her brother Paolo could come and go as he pleased. It wasn't fair, but there was little point in feeling sorry for herself since the other girls her age lived by the same rules in their homes.

"When you are ready to get married, we'll find the right man. You don't need to worry about it," her father said.

It was bad enough that her father felt this way, but without her mother in her corner, she'd never have the life she'd always dreamed about. She wanted to wait to marry—to wait until she fell in love.

"Love? You'll be lucky to find a good man, a good provider. Love will come later," her mother insisted.

When an opportunity to come to America with friends presented, Ciara jumped at the chance to change her future. If she stayed in Gaeta, she'd never meet the man she would fall in love with. She knew all the boys in her part of the world, and no one had caught her eye. To her, they were all the same and she could expect them to adhere to the same rules and traditions that she had been groomed to accept without question.

It was a brave and risky move. Her parents disowned her the minute she told them what she intended to do.

"You are not our daughter anymore," her mother and father yelled as Ciara walked away from the only home she'd ever known. Only Paolo, her brother, ran after her. He handed her several hundred euro that he had saved.

"No, Paolo. I cannot take this."

"Don't argue with me, Ciara. Take this money, and as soon as I can, I will come to join you in America."

She took the money and hugged him tight. A car with two women inside pulled up next to her and she got in. As it pulled away, Ciara leaned out the window and waved to Paolo.

She learned to speak English, went out with her two friends from Italy and met a few new ones. She waitressed at a restaurant on Sanibel Island and found a tiny apartment near her work.

Paolo kept his promise and joined his sister in Sanibel, Florida. They built a thriving plant nursery and worked on the island of Captiva for an elderly woman who needed help inside and outside her property. Rose Johnson Lane had become a second mother to Ciara and Paolo, and they found a permanent home in the southwest part of Florida.

They travelled back to Gaeta a few times over the years. Her parents had softened their position. In their eyes, Paolo would not only look after her but would now become the head of the family even if the family was beyond the Atlantic. Ciara laughed at her parents' old ways that would never change and chose to love them regardless.

Ciara loved living in Florida. Her life was full caring for others and working alongside her brother. But her dream of finding someone to love and build a life with was beyond her reach. She'd dated a few men over the years, but no one captured her heart. She'd resigned herself to never marry and had all but given up when an email popped up in her inbox from Maurizio Bianchi, the son of her family's enemy.

Ciara knew she should ignore the email and never mention it to her brother, but it seemed innocent enough to read it and decide on her own what to do. She remembered Maurizio as the handsome young son of Gustavo Bianchi, but she didn't know much about him and never made eye contact with him whenever she saw him.

His email surprised her, and she found it difficult to understand why Maurizio, of all people, would be the one to update her on her mother and father's health. How he even knew such details didn't confuse her since their town was small and news of anyone living there traveled quickly. It was that he went to so much trouble to get her email address. That action alone impressed Ciara and the moment she hit the send button on her response, she was giddy with anticipation.

It was the beginning of a months-long communication that started as a friendship and in time, a romance. She never said a word to Paolo about her correspondence with Maurizio, until her new love wanted to come to America and be with her. As much as she knew how her brother would respond, she had no choice but to go to him and explain. She was in love, finally. Nothing would stand in her way of happiness after all this time.

But she was wrong. Paolo forbid Maurizio's coming to Captiva, and even worse, her correspondence with him. Ciara refused to accept her brother's position. It was the twenty-first century after all. She didn't leave Gaeta only to be left with little choice about how she would live her life in America.

Maggie Wheeler was now her sister-in-law, and someone who believed differently than her husband. She supported Ciara and Maurizio's relationship and would help her find a way to bring Maurizio to America with Paolo's support.

Ciara had lived her life without the warmth of a man's arms around her. She'd given up on a future with children. Now, her dream of a family of her own and the security of having someone to grow old with was within reach. How Maggie would manage such a miracle, Ciara didn't know. But she'd place her faith in the power of love, and the support of family. Two things that she believed in with all her heart.

A NOTE FROM THE AUTHOR

Thank you so much for reading
CAPTIVA CHRISTMAS.

THE CAPTIVA ISLAND SERIES
Where you will meet The Wheeler Family and a cast of unforgettable characters you will fall in love with.

Book Five in this series:
CAPTIVA NIGHTS
Will release February 2023.

Check out the other books in this series:

Book One: KEY LIME GARDEN INN
Book Two: A CAPTIVA WEDDING
Book Three: CAPTIVA MEMORIES

ACKNOWLEDGMENTS

A huge thank you to Lisa Lee of Lisa Lee Proofreading and Editing. I'm forever grateful that we found each other.

To Anne Marie Page Cooke, thank you for agreeing to read and reread my books. It's been so much fun having you to talk to as this book develops.

To Marianne Nowicki of Premade Ebook Cover Shop. The cover of Captiva Christmas is beautiful and I have to acknowledge your patience with me throughout the year as I kept changing things at the last minute.

To my friends and family who have supported me and cheered me on from the beginning. I love you all.

To my sweet husband who continues to be the first person to read the books I write. Your perspective means so much to me. I love you.

To my readers: Thank you for your continued support and kind words. 2022 has been an amazing year and I hope you are looking forward to 2023 as much as I am. I have so much more to say in my stories. Thank you for coming along on this journey with me.

Blessing dear friends.

Annie

ABOUT THE AUTHOR

Annie Cabot is the author of contemporary women's fiction and family sagas. Annie writes about friendships and family relationships, that bring inspiration and hope to others.

Annie Cabot is the pen name for the writer Patricia Pauletti (Patti) who, for the last seven years, has been the co-author of several paranormal mystery books under the pen name Juliette Harper. A lover of all things happily ever after, it was only a matter of time before she began to write what was in her heart, and so, the pen name Annie Cabot was born.

When she's not writing, Annie and her husband like to travel. Winters always involve time away on Captiva Island, Florida where she continues to get inspiration for her novels.

Annie lives in Massachusetts with her husband and furbaby Otis.

For more information visit anniecabot.com

Made in the USA
Middletown, DE
02 July 2023